MW01098745

Published by Writer's Publishing House

https://writerspublishinghouse.com

Cover credited by Writer's Publishing House Staff

Interior Layout – Writer's Publishing House Staff

By Alborz Azar

https://alborzazar.net

ISBN - 9781952274022

Disclaimer

The author has made every effort to ensure the accuracy of the information within this book was correct at time of publication. The author does not assume and hereby disclaims any liability to any party for any loss, damage, or disruption caused by errors or omissions, whether such errors or omissions result from accident, negligence, or any other cause.

The information contained within this Book/eBook is strictly for educational purposes. If you wish to apply ideas contained in this Book/eBook, you are taking full responsibility for your actions.

Disclaimer: The Publisher and the Author make no representation or warranties with respect to the accuracy or completeness of the contents of this work and specifically disclaim all warranties for a particular purpose. No warranty may be created or extended by sales or promotional materials. The advice and strategies contained herein may not be suitable for every situation. This work is sold with the understanding that the Publisher is not engaged in rendering legal, accounting, or other professional services. If professional assistance is required, the services of a competent professional person should be sought. Neither the Publisher nor the Author shall be liable for damages arising therefrom.

The fact that an organization or website is referred to in this work as a citation and/or potential source of further information does not mean that the Author or the Publisher endorses the information, the organization, or website it may provide or recommendations it may make. Further, readers should be aware that websites listed in this work may have changed or disappeared between when this work was written and when it is read.

The cases and stories in this book have had details changed to preserve privacy.

The RAHA Series – Book One

WHO DID IIT

By Alborz Azar

Acknowledgments

I wish Eshgham the best of luck for inspiring me to start writing in April 2018. "WHO DID IIT" is the first book that was completed in 2019.

The book is dedicated to Pantea. All efforts have been made to write this memoir with inspiration from the true story of Pantea (now 41 years) and Alborz (now 66 years); who loved this woman more than words can express. As the prose states, he would have done anything for Pantea's happiness, even it meant dying in her honor.

Alborz discovered Pantea was a one of a kind individual in her wisdom of the world. She has unmatchable charm, unlike any other girl on the planet. She is truly one in a billion.

I give my sincere thanks to Lizzy McNett, who has worked so hard in helping to complete this book. I appreciated all her patience, and efforts to edit the words and help me publish the series that contains the story of my life.

"Pantea if you had not been brought into my life, there would be no story to write this book." -Alborz

It is my sincerest hope the readers enjoy the story of my life. Thank you for purchasing this book. Please, continue reading on to experience the saga.

Table of Contents

Chapter One:

She Turned to Pimping

I was twenty-three years old when I met a beautiful girl; she was fifteen. We dated for three years until she was of legal age and then we got married in court. However, later her parents set up an arranged marriage as per the ritual within thirty days with various conditions. There would be no dowry, etc., and I had no problem with that since I just wanted the girl. We have been happily married for forty years, with four children; three daughters and one son were born when I was forty-two.

My business dealings were exporting products around the world. On one trip to Milan when I was thirty, we were looking for some machines. A business friend, Kumar, came along for the purchasing; he made a call to have a girl visit my hotel room. I had never been outside of my marriage to Rozhan, my wife. After the trip back to India, my friend Kumar called for another girl to see me at a hotel, she was a sweet girl. The meeting led to an introduction to her pimp who dealt with high-profile call girls and high-profile businessmen, and politicians.

My interludes extended to once a week for a few hours, a different girl each time and different times of the day. But I want to mention that I had a very satisfactory sex life with my wife, who never knew about my sex outside our marriage.

I became frustrated as the call girls could not fulfill my needs or expectations. I only met with four good girls but was looking for one person to meet once a week regularly. On one incident, I met a girl who was with another girl whom I liked. Her name was Rupali. She had come specifically to meet a minister, and I did not get the opportunity to stay with her. My stint lasted from 1983 to 1999 before I met the right girl who introduced herself as Aafree, whom I found through the same pimp. My schedule didn't allow me to be with her that day, so we arranged a meet up the next evening. I was very impressed; she was of the Parsi religion, beautiful, stylish, my perfect match.

Our scheduled meeting the next day went badly because she never showed. Out of frustration, I called the pimp and shouted about my frustration. I demanded to have the girl's contact number, but her phone went straight to voicemail. The pimp informed she lived in Mumbai. I was so attracted to the girl I made an excuse at home so I could fly to Bombay the same evening. After my arrival, there was still no answer. I left several messages in hopes she'd call back soon. In the meantime, I met with another girl. She met me at the airport and we went to the Sun and Sand Hotel in Juhu, Bombay. The girl was not to my liking since my mind was on Aafree and I wanted to meet her again. Rupali came with her pimp, since we missed each other the night before, because of her engagement with a prominent minister. It was just my good luck; she was good, but I told her about Aafree who had come to see me. Then at about 11 pm, the hotel phone rang, and to my surprise it was Aafree. I was excited to hear from her.

I set our meeting for the next day and asked to meet once a week for 1,000 dollars a night. Aafree was needy and greedy; I expressed the desire to meet her for 24 hours to 48 hours a week. "I am looking for roti kapda makan," she said (this means "food, clothes and a house").

"I promise all that in time, but we need to spend some time together first."

After that, we met every week, sometimes for two days. She claimed to be twenty-eight, which never bothered me since our time was excellent. We had been together for three years when she disclosed, she was divorced and had two sons: one fifteen and the other eighteen. Both lived in Canada with their father. The news didn't bother me; even when she revealed her real age was thirty-nine, it was irrelevant. Later, I met her sons when they came to stay at the hotels. They were fond of me. We traveled all over Europe, the USA, Hong Kong, and other countries. At times her sons traveled with us. We partied at many pubs, nightclubs, etc. However, part of our agreement was that she would leave the call girl scene, but this didn't happen. I understood the reason, except she lied. She would deny the phone calls and meet with various clients through pimps, and later she herself started pimp work. We had many discussions about doing the pimp work, and it was something I asked her to stop. Our relationship lasted for ten years, and I took excellent care of Aafree.

I bought her a house, a car, and later built another floor on the same bungalow. Although it was about a 100 sq. meter plot, I spent about 400,0000 dollars on it besides buying the plot. After several years, when her own pimp work flourished, and she was busy with calls, it annoyed me. I warned her over the next three years that she would lose me, but my alerts went unnoticed. I even promised to stay faithful and not fuck around with anyone else.

The problem escalated. During our meetings, Aafree stared bringing girls, and she wanted me to find friends who would meet with them. The whole situation upset me a great deal, but I wanted to be with her and was not looking for anyone else.

One meeting, on my birthday 2011 when I had already been with Aafree for twelve years, she arranged an Indian Mujra (Indian dance) by a girl by the name of Seema. She was lovely and an excellent dancer. When I flew back to Delhi the next day, Seema called to say she had left a watch in the room. I informed her there was no watch in my room. Anyway, I offered to come and see her performance in Chandigarh someday. She liked the idea and agreed to come with another girl performer. We met, and I asked her if she would like to have sex for extra money, and she agreed. We had a good time; both girls performed very well in their dances. Seema was very young but very enticing. She met with me in Chandigarh at my presidential suite. Of course, I had sex with her, although she was very young. But Seema had a beautiful body and was full of youth. Nonetheless, she had a boyfriend. I convinced her to meet with me occasionally; however, this relationship was temporary. I was looking for a long-term situation. We met a few times and eventually became good friends. I purchased a very small flat for her in Delhi and then had it put in her name. I did this to reward her for helping me to try to get free of Aafree.

Aafree and I were meeting regularly, but I was looking for a replacement. Her pimp business had taken over her life. It was a frustrating disappointment. But finding someone else was hard, and the last thing I wanted was one night stands.

Chapter Two:

It was Love at First Sight

On July 12, 2012, I had a matter in the Supreme Court to attend, but Aafree and I were meeting after the engagement. She would stay in a hotel at Friends Colony, one suite for us and a room for Lana, another girl. Aafree informed me of both room numbers and said we were in 166. Then, she told me if my officer friend, Amar wanted to be with the girl he could for a few hours; she would charge 500 dollars. I confirmed with Amar and arranged with him to come by around 7 p.m.

I arrived around 5, earlier than expected. But when I entered the room, it was occupied. To my utter surprise, a man was on top of a naked girl. Aafree apologized that she gave me the wrong room number. I should have gone to 162, and we laughed about the mix-up.

Shortly after the incident, the phone rang. Lana was distraught over the experience. She explained it was Alborz, her boyfriend. Aafree gave me the wrong room number, but the explanation did not console her. So, she sent Sunny out of the hotel room. Once she calmed down, we convinced her of the mistake and she finished the session with my friend Amar. Then, she came back to our room with a portable music system; we listened to some excellent music. Lana, the girl, danced with my friend. Then, I asked her to dance with me. I asked permission from Aafree and she complied. During our encounter, Lana insisted on dancing close. I whispered that Aafree would not approve. But I put my hand around her waist while we danced. She was excellent in her nature, and I fell in love on the spot.

Since I was looking for a change, the notion of pursuing a relationship was open. I had not been happy over the last three years because of Aafree's pimp work. In the previous year, per Aafree's arrangement, on my birthday, I had met Seema a few times.

In between the meetings, I sought Rupali, who agreed to meet when I asked. Unlike Aafree, Rupali was always crazy to meet; she liked me. We had sex. But the day I met

Lana after my Supreme Court case; it was a lucky day. It introduced me to my dream girl and I wanted her for the rest of my life. It was love at first sight, like with Rozhan, my wife.

Lana was on a student visa. She was a Persian from Iran and had spoken with Aafree about the visa issue. We talked about her zodiac sign; she was an Aries. The fire signs were always my favorite. My wife Rozhan is a Leo, and Aafree is a Sagittarius, all fiery zodiac signs. Besides, I was a number 1 as I was born on the 19th. I was always attracted to numbers. One or four similarly, Aafree was a number 1 born on the 10th of December, my wife was born on the 31st making her a 4, and Lana was born on the 4th making her a number 4, and on top of that, she was born in the 4th month.

Aafree assured Lana could trust me, that I could help her in getting a visa. But she did not enjoy discussing the matter. We were meeting the next day, so I decided to speak about the issue again. But to my surprise, when I arrived, Aafree told me Lana had left that morning on a flight at six a.m. It was imperative I get her phone number somehow, but it was out of the question to ask Aafree. My next thought was to get July's phone bill from Aafree. Unfortunately, I could not get her phone bill.

However, my luck improved. It was our anniversary on the twenty-third of August, and we used to meet for two days. As usual, she brought a girl along. We were staying in a presidential suite that had two bedrooms. While we were talking, Aafree got a message from a client. For the first time in thirteen years, she handed me her phone and said if another client calls, I should have them attend. Destiny shined down on me. I immediately searched for Lana's cell number and BBM pin. I connected with her by sending an invitation on BBM immediately, and she accepted the invite.

I sent her message the same day on August 23, 2012. My message read, "Are Aries confidential?"

She replied, "Yes, but why?"

"We met through Aafree. Can we meet without letting Aafree know?"

"Yes," she agreed.

I immediately suggested September 1st in Hyderabad for two nights. Then we discussed the amount. I offered 1,000 dollars each night.

She said, "But baby, it's for two nights and that is a lot of time. Give me 1,500 dollars a night."

"But this will be a continuous appointment. So, it would be 2,000 dollars." My offer was the same as Aafree's payment for the last thirteen years. She agreed. Lana had some things going for her, which will be revealed in later chapters.

Aafree had upset me over the last three years with her pimp work. Although, my love for her was intense. I told her many times that one day I would elope, and the time came on August 23, 2012. I opened an account for Aafree at Indus Bank. We had been together for a long time, so I felt obligated to give her something. I deposited 28,000 dollars, which was two percent of the amount I made from my business work. Aafree was very greedy; I kept the reasoning to myself.

To my surprise again, Aafree left on August 24, 2012, after she got the 28,000 dollars from me, and didn't inform me she was meeting with her son in Canada. Another situation that annoyed me was her constant secrets and lies. She was staying for a month, which I did not know about until two days later. It gave me the opportunity to meet Lana without concern over Aafree's presence. We planned to meet on

September 1, 2012, in Hyderabad. I booked her flight and mine. We stayed at Taj Faluknama Palace, a grand luxury suite. My luggage was filled with cosmetics and perfumes from Delhi. It was my first meeting with Lana. A minimum purchase could have been 2,000 dollars, but it came to 4,000 dollars and I knew deep down it was a chance to build our romance. I do not know the reason for my certainty.

I arrived early to set up the room with flowers and gifts, as usual. Prior arrangements were made to pick Lana up at the airport. I told her to look for a driver in a blue shirt, which was me. I was apprehensive about seeing her again and wasn't sure if we were still compatible.

My choice of girls has always been stringent. I needed to make sure they were a good fit. Once I saw Lana walking out of the terminal exit, I was impressed and knew immediately she was the right choice. We shook hands and headed for the hotel. Since I had booked her travel ticket, as it was a custom that the client arranged the air ticket, I knew her real name was Pantea and not Lana.

Further conversation led to age, and she told me she was thirty-four. I was comfortable since my taste was not in young women. Although, she looked to be twenty-five. At this point, she passed two tests.

The Faluknama Palace is a royal hotel, and they transport their guests around by horse and buggy. It was exciting, especially for me, as I enjoyed treating the girls with tender loving care. Once we arrived at our room, the hotel staff took a photo of us on the balcony. At this point, we were showered with rose petals as we walked to our room. It made us feel like a king and queen. The grand luxury suite welcomed us with chocolate cake and candles. I told Lana we must cut it together since it was our anniversary: our first official meeting.

We sat for hours and talked about ourselves. I wanted to be completely honest, so I informed her of my criminal case pending in court. Lana panicked and started searching for my name on Google. She thought I was a murderer or a serious, heinous criminal. We discussed the problems, and that they had to do with my company. She said, "So, what? It is very common." It gave me further confidence that she passed two more tests. Her innocence and acceptance of me were great. The frivolous criminal case was for the government to use me as a scapegoat. It will be detailed in another book.

Our lovemaking brought up one red flag when I found out she made many sounds while having sex. She explained that clients like it this way. Later, the conversation continued, and we discussed my plan to see her exclusively. I would take care of her, but she did not have to give up her other clients until she felt secure with our arrangement.

Lana was so impressed by my honesty and only wanting to see one girl. Most men jump around to different women regularly. Lana was surprised that I had been with Aafree for thirteen years. In fact, I realized she was not a professional call girl; she was too simple, too straightforward, clean-hearted, intelligent, knowledgeable, beautiful, and excellent in bed. She was a good girl that was not greedy, nor did she want to continue this profession. We agreed to 100/100 marks, since I had found someone to spend the rest of my life with. I knew one day she would leave this work and stay with me and trust me. It took a few months, but she did. Our first meeting was going better than I ever imagined. It was time to shower her with gifts, and she was very excited by the cosmetics and perfumes.

She gave me an unexpected kiss, "I love surprises." Her happiness made me feel comfortable with my decision.

Evening set in by this time, and I was ready for a beer. I offered Lana a drink, and she had vodka, Roberto Cavalli. We drank for several hours and decided on some snacks. The room service brought us a plethora of options. After eating until our cravings were satisfied, we went down to the nightclub. I drank a beer and Lana had a Gray Goose.

The crowd in the nightclub was loud and not to our liking, so we departed for our room. We made love for several hours. I had fallen in love, but for her, I was just a client.

It was a custom for me not to fall asleep right away and to save time for talking. I was excited she agreed, so I jumped up with excitement. In doing so, a fart came out. We laughed at my flatulence.

Later Lana admitted she had accepted the BBM invitation by mistake as though it was from Alborz. She said, "We met at a party a few months back and I was very drunk when your BBM invite came."

After accepting my BBM invite it surprised her of the meeting in Delhi as Aafree's boyfriend. Most girls in this business don't have boyfriends, so it surprised her when I asked to meet. The conversation ended, and we slept well together. But the morning hangover was unusual; it seems the club's vodka was spurious.

The royal breakfast was incredible as always. Lana just drank coffee, but I had a traditional South Indian meal, Idli Dosa. I took care of her for the entire day. Lana did not drink much, but I had my usual beer that I always brought with me, as I don't care for Indian brewed beer.

Our evening turned out to be mind-blowing: The sex was incredible, although for me it was love. Lana passed all the tests. I asked her if we could enter a ten-year oral contract to meet as often as possible.

Her favorite comment was "Let's see. All the clients want the girl to be theirs only and to take complete care of them. But, since most of the clients are with a different girl all the time, how can this be possible?"

Lana continued to talk and ask about Aafree. I explained our relationship lasted a long time and I loved her, so leaving her was not an option. Our departure the next day was upsetting. I didn't want her to leave, but we arranged for another meeting. She would come to Chandigarh. I waited until she boarded the plane, which was a foreign concept to Lana. Most men left her at the gate. I felt it was important to take care of the girls completely.

Her acceptance to meet me again meant she was happy, although for me it had turned into true love. It was the beginning of my next love affair after Aafree. It was also the first meeting with a lovely, beautiful girl who was out of my league.

Chapter Three:

She Danced and Sang

We met again two days later at the JW Marriott Chandigarh, in the Presidential Suite. It was such a lovely feeling meeting with her again; I was really falling in love.

We talked for hours and later took a bath together. She was direct and to the point. Plus, she loved to play the game Angry Birds. I enjoyed every moment. One night I played some music for her called o merae sanam doe jism magar ik jaan hae hum - "We are two bodies but one life." It was my favorite song. She always teased me after that, my o merae sanam.

We were getting along so well; my dreams were coming true. I felt comfortable with Lana, but she was Pantea to me as her real name was Pantea. So, I decided to ask for some assistance. "If an officer wanted to meet someone, would you be able to arrange something?"

"Yes, I can," she agreed.

A call was placed to set up a meeting with someone from Iran; she charged 1,000 dollars per night. I agreed.

The first night would be with someone she did not know, but the second evening would be a guy we had met on the 12th of July with me and Aafree.

Our stay lasted two days in Chandigarh, then we left for Delhi. I booked a presidential suite at the Taj Mahal Hotel. Her friend Leela came. Both of them sounded very close and were happy to be together. I met my officer friend Mohammed in the lobby and escorted him into the room. He was impressed by the suite.

My friend and I were talking when the two gorgeous girls came out of the bedroom. He was stunned by their beauty. I introduced Lana as my girlfriend. The conversation made him feel comfortable.

Lana was good, straightforward, simple, and easygoing; I watched her closely. While dancing, she sang, Atif Aslam's song in Hindi, although she didn't know Hindi. She was dancing to a song called Subha honae na de tu mera hero ("Let morning not come, you are my hero"). Her confession of loving to dance was amazing. She could dance to this song even in her sleep. Both girls undid the officer's shirt along with mine, and we danced on the dining room table. It was a lovely evening and we all had a great time. At about 2 am, my friend was happy with Leela and retired to a private room. Once they left, Pantea satisfied me unbelievably. The morning was just as unexplainable. Her beauty was uncompromising; she was a blessing in my life.

We spent two days together, and we had already been in each other's company for the last four days. I grew closer and closer to Lana during this time and was falling deeper in love. From that day forward, I never called her Lana again. Pantea was becoming an essential part of my life.

The next morning, I was in the living room while she was still sleeping, and I happened to see her phone on the table. A text came through and the heading read, "Lana, I know you are annoyed. Why aren't you responding? You are still here and have not gone back to your country."

It didn't bother me as I knew she was a call girl. Her clients must be missing her; she was beautiful. Pantea was her given name as a call girl. I never liked it anyway.

As Pantea had curly hair during this meeting but in Chandigarh it was straight, I wondered if my officer friend Amar would recognize the girl with straight hair. It had been two months, but he recognized her immediately. I explained she was mine and Leela was coming to see him. The arrangement was agreeable. We had a nice evening as usual.

My friend, however, was clumsy and broke an expensive table lamp which we had to pay to replace. Then, he wanted to have sex multiple times with Leela, like every hour. "My friend is not a machine," Pantea explained.

"I agree. I will compensate her for the situation."

We had been together for the last six nights in seven days, and I had to make excuses at home. Over the last two days at the Taj Delhi, the bill was 6,000 dollars, but I was so happy and satisfied with Pantea I was fine with spending all that money. I found someone of my choice and begun a fresh new life. I decided to satisfy Pantea with so much money she would leave call girl work and become mine exclusively. However, I would never ask her to leave the work. I was sure she didn't like her work and would be very happy to stay with me.

However, every time I asked her, she would say, "Let's see."

My confidence grew daily that she would eventually stay with me alone, since I was in love as a man, not a client. I committed to her for the first ten years, and thereafter we would decide if another ten years or twenty years was possible. So, I prepared mentally for ten years until 2022, when readers will know whether my true love will prevail over her belief of "Let's see" or not.

Chapter Four:

It Was Fate

Pantea and I continued to meet every week regularly for
one to two nights depending on our schedules. We were
becoming more intimate. She was on a student visa,
and many times had college work to complete. It was
difficult for her, but to stay in India she had to go through
some major hardships.

September 2012 was our first month together. During the
second week, she informed me that she was leaving to visit
her parents in Iran. So, I offered to fly to Mumbai and see
her off at the airport. Pantea got very upset on the phone: "I
am not a buccha (child)." It was a pet word.

She told me later that since she had a student visa, no one
would rent her a flat. Additionally, before she left, she had
to vacate her current flat and find somewhere else to live.
Plus, her visa was from Pune and not Mumbai. Pantea hung
up the phone in an angered state. The situation left me

concerned for her situation and I called back to explain, "I will fly in and come to buy you a flat. You can move along with having a place for your things."

She replied, "But what about police verification? I don't want to get them involved."

"You will not need verification. I will take care of everything." She just could not believe I could help her that easily.

She immediately called her two friends Leela and Milin, asking, "Do you think a client that I only met three weeks ago would really risk putting up a call girl in his flat? Plus, make this happen in three days?"

In any case, her favorite expression was "Let's see," and she left it at that. Over the phone, "I have three days to get this done, how on Earth is this possible?" she shouted in her own way.

I was committed to Pantea and always believed in targeting my goals. The size of the task doesn't matter if you believe. I searched the newspapers and found three apartments. It was a difficult decision since I am very fussy and did not know her taste. We had only met three weeks ago, but luck was on my side. I found a woman who was a property

broker in the area Pantea wanted to live. I arranged
an appointment. I left the next day for Mumbai to search
for and select an acceptable flat for Pantea. I had fallen in
love with a call girl, not by choice; rather, I couldn't
believe it, since a call girl's normal job was to use men. I
kept assuring myself in my heart of hearts that she was not
that way with me. I had nothing to worry about. I needed to
make sure she was completely satisfied with everything she
needed in her life.

I asked Pantea to meet me at 9 a.m. Since her party habits
demanded the nights, nine was early. However, she made
the time. We looked at three apartments and did not like
any of them. I realized she had good taste. It was not out of
greed; she wanted a place where she could feel at home and
comfortable. Plus, she wanted to be in an area that was safe
since she lived alone.

Our next appointment was promising. We met the property
broker at 2 p.m. after eating lunch at the JW Marriott. We
looked for the next four hours and rejected most of the
flats. Pantea and I were in sync with our choices, and that
made me happy. Finally, we saw one at Savgan Society,
an apartment in the area Pantea wanted. We both agreed on
the building and flat. Fate was on our side; she informed

me later that she had already seen the flat available for rent, but being a foreigner and a single woman, they would not rent to her.

I discussed the price with the broker and set the deal at 222,2000 dollars since the owner wanted 266,0000 dollars. I made an appointment to meet the broker in the morning and pay the full price. I needed it to be registered by the next day, as my girlfriend had to be out of her current residence in three days. The next day we met, and whatever price the seller agreed to I immediately accepted, since I wanted to get Pantea the flat and then return to Delhi.

Somehow, I was able to register the sale deeds in a day and give Pantea her keys to move to her new flat. She was stunned by the results, but I was only looking out for her comfort. My motives were selfless. Anyway, I sorted out all the problems; and was able to furnish the flat beautifully at my expense. Pantea was able to make a home for herself there. Now it did not require police verification, so there was no more stress for her.

Pantea promised we could make love one day in her apartment. I did visit after she finished decorating, but told her it looked like a baby's apartment: "I would NOT like to have sex here."

She appreciated my feeling and kissed me. "Where were you three years ago? If we'd known each other, I would not have fallen into the shit work that I hate."

I felt so happy about her sentiment and knew someday she would be with me exclusively.

Chapter Five

A Great Opportunity

My meetings with Pantea continued twice a week; we were growing closer. I had truly fallen in love with her. During each encounter, she added more detail on how she became a call girl, which she referred to as her 'work'. Pantea came from a wealthy family in Iran. Her father was a professor and a well-known personality. He was retired, but also a miser.

Her relationship with her mother is different; she loves her. Saba, her sister, committed suicide but had been married to Arash. The situation was tragic before her passing: She wanted to meet with Pantea, but for some reason, she was unable to. Pantea often cried when talking about her sister, who she loved very much. After two years, the pain was still fresh.

Pantea has a younger brother who was twenty at the time we met. However, the only one she genuinely loved was her mother.

As I understand it, she has had many boyfriends but never stayed with anyone for very long. She always cheated on them. Her longest relationship lasted for three years with a boy named Iman from Iran, with whom she lived in an apartment in Juhu. He organized a business visa for her by incorporating a company called Pasard Private Limited where she was made a director to get an Indian visa. He was a fitness trainer.

Pantea said he was crazy about her and wanted to get married. His family was wealthy, and she lived with him for three years in Juhu. The initial visa was renewed for two years in India. Her boyfriend managed all her work.

Within the first month of arriving in India, she was in Poona at the FRRO office. A girl was watching her fill out the form, and she asked whether Pantea needed help. She said yes, and she introduced herself. This was Milin who was also from Iran. She gave Pantea her phone number and said that if she ever needed money, she could do dance shows through an event company for 200 dollars. Pantea agreed and started doing shows one month later since she didn't want to ask for any money from her father. She would make about 200 dollars for four recitals, but she preferred to party at the nightclubs with her friends and spend all her money.

Per the advice of her friend, Pantea began doing some dance performances and started to make some money. Then one day, she was invited to a party in a suite. They were call girls, but she was the ballet dancer.

They asked her, "Why you don't work for Lorryl?" The famous high-profile pimp was a Russian girl. At first, Pantea hesitated to call her, but due to the expenses of partying, she contacted Lorryl. They discussed the pay scale, which was fifty percent of the work. She discussed this with Milin too before calling Lorryl but Milin was hesitant. Later, Pantea also got Milin into this work.

Pantea continued to explain, "We met with two to three men a day, but I didn't want to meet with these men any longer. I started drinking before the appointments. The pay totaled 600 dollars to 800 dollars for a short time, sometimes even less than two hours. At times, I was able to save 60,000 dollars and sent it to Iran to my savings."

The clients quickly grew fond of her and some of them wanted to meet every week for a few hours. She would come back on an early flight the next morning. The Trident Hotel in Mumbai was Pantea's favorite place to stay. After work, she'd party at the China House at the Grand Hyatt. The desk attendants always said, "Welcome back, ma'am."

Pantea kept her new career choice from her boyfriend. It caused a rift in their relationship. During any confrontation she denied everything, and she shouted back to shut him up. The situation remained stable until she came home one day from a shopping spree. The bags were filled with expensive lingerie. He asked where she got the money to buy these items. "From shows," she told him. Of course, he didn't believe the explanation but stayed quiet.

"He begged me to marry him many times, but I was not into marriage," she stated.

The situation caused her boyfriend to worry, and when he told her she was heading down the wrong path she scoffed at his comments.

She always said, "I do not believe in love. What is love? Can you define it?"

I told her, "Love is when someone does everything for the other person no matter what."

Her reply was, "Okay, if I asked you to jump out a window, would you?"

I said, "Yes, I would."

"But you have a family and children, so why would you jump for me?" I would have jumped.

My love was true and I would have even done it just to make her happy. I believed the day would come when she'd say, "I love you."

Pantea knew very high-profile people from parties but kept everything with her work discreet. When we met, she would enter the hotel room by herself and refused to go alone with me to any restaurants. Whatever we did had to happen in our room, which was the opposite of what I liked.

Pantea's self-respect was important, and her mannerisms always amazed me. She was a soft-hearted, straightforward, well-mannered girl. She always impressed me when she dressed up. Our relationship developed a lot over the first two years. Sometimes she would get angry and shout for no reason, but she always thought about her actions and apologized later in her own way or would feel guilty by herself. Nonetheless, I love her for the person she is inside. I believed she could become much more with someone in her life that truly cared.

It was difficult at times since we had to keep our relationship behind closed doors. I loved to party and did so with Aafree, but Pantea refused to be seen with me in public.

We'd met for two months for a total of twenty nights and thirty days. I was crazily making excuses at home and for court dates, etc.

I had been buying Pantea gifts but had her do the shopping. I wanted her to feel comfortable and happy with me. In these two months, she made 20,000 dollars from me. If she was busy, it meant less time to see any other clients, which in any case had been reduced to almost nil.

Pantea was not fooling anyone; she enjoyed spending time with me. We had no binding contract and either one of us could leave at any time, except for my personal agreement to stay with her for ten years.

She always reminded me, "Baby...I won't be here for ten years. After my boyfriend left me, he went back to Iran and got married. I had no business to back up my visa.

Once it expired, my student visa took its place. That will expire in one year, it cannot be extended again."

At that point, Aafree came back from Canada. We spent time together as well. Pantea was aware of our meetings, but she did not say a word. By this time, I had fallen in love and wanted to be with Pantea. I needed to find a way to leave Aafree, and an opportunity would present itself soon.

Chapter Six:

My Love Drove Me

I continued to meet with both girls separately but divided my time between Aafree and Pantea, as well as with my work and family. Since Aafree was more concerned about her pimp job, we only met about four days a month. We usually met in Delhi for one day until midnight, and then I'd go home. With Pantea we always spent one night together. My love drove me to spend as much time with her as possible. Especially overnight, although that was not her favorite. I loved to sleep holding her hand for some time.

On her phone, she saved my name as Chipkoo (stuck all the time). I saw her phone one day when she got a call from a friend; I happened to glance at it when a call came in and saw she had Chipkoo 1 and Chipkoo 2.

I asked, "Who is Chipkoo number 2?"

"You… since you have two cell numbers." It made me happy to know I was the only Chipkoo.

Aafree was always too busy during our time together and was constantly on the phone or laptop. Her pimp job was making her enormous amounts of money. She stopped making time for just us, which had been part of the problem for many years. Pantea, on the other hand, always had her mind and body with me. I was enjoying her company to the fullest. At times, she had other things come up, but that was to be expected.

One day I told Pantea about Rupali's story. She said, "Please invite her next time we are in Mumbai."

I used to always discuss everything about Aafree with Rupali as we were very close friends. We used to have lunch and discuss each other's lives, including Rupali's boyfriend, Kartil who was also married but knew we were meeting. On one occasion, Rupali visited the Leela Hotel to see Seema's performance.

I was with Seema the night Rupali told me, "Alborz you should try to avoid these Mujra girls." She had a friend who had been ruined by a Mujra dancer as he was constantly lying around drunk in her house. But I didn't like her criticizing Seema. She was a fire sign, Leo, worth trusting. On the second day, I spent the night with Rupali. All of this happened before I met Pantea during the period when I was fed up with Aafree. In any case, Aafree knew Rupali since both of them had been to Kenya and knew some of Aafree's clients.

I discussed everything about Pantea with Rupali. We hid nothing; I was always a comfortable confidante. Per Pantea, I agreed to invite Rupali, who met us for dinner at the Hyatt presidential suite. Incidentally, a colleague from America, the president of a bank, called me to meet Mr. Ajay from Switzerland. He was in India working with a big finance company. He suggested that he could help me deal with some huge financial issues. The project concerned my two five-star hotel projects that were stuck in litigation with the government.

I replied, "I am in Mumbai right now, but he can come to meet with me today at the Hyatt." I asked Pantea to call Rupali to see if she was comfortable having someone else join us. Ajay arrived after Rupali.

Rupali agreed with Pantea's nature. The girls appreciated, each other. Thereafter, we met several times for drinks together.

I introduced Pantea to Ajay as my girlfriend and Rupali as a friend. Ajay was eyeing Rupali, and I didn't like the ogling, even though he was a well-educated, nice guy. Ajay and I moved to a separate table to discuss work issues. He understood my eagerness to leave after our conversation ended.

We started our evening plans. The girls pushed me into performing a striptease on top of the dining table, but I did not take off my underwear. We partied in the suite until 3 am when Rupali left. Pantea and I made love, but during our pillow talk, she revealed something: "Alborz… I miss my mom."

"You must go visit her right away. I'll arrange for your trip." We slept late the next day. I reminded her of our conversation and made arrangements for her to travel on December 17th.

Pantea asked if I was still seeing Aafree. "I have seen her a few times, but since we have been together for thirteen years that may not change." We discussed everything I had done for her over the years.

Pantea wrote me a lovely one-line note on a 100-dollar bill. It read, "Alborz, you are the best striptease dancer I have ever seen." She signed it Boos (kisses) in Persian.

I told her Aafree's birthday was coming up on December 10th and we always celebrated in a posh manner. "Would you like to come?" I asked. "I could ask Aafree to invite you. We will be in the presidential suite at the Hyatt."

"No… I will not come. It will be embarrassing."

I still told Aafree to invite her on December 10th, as she had invited twenty of her girlfriends and her son Herol and a few of his friends.

Pantea declined. "I am busy."

As usual, it was a lovely birthday party, well organized. I always went all out for her birthday. We had thirty girls, Herol and his two friends. We had a great time with Sheesha, only the best quality liquor, and lavish food, and the girls, as usual, were attracted to me since I am hospitable and looked after them well. The party made me realize how much I missed Pantea. I didn't want to look at anyone else; I had found my true love. My relationship with Aafree was over; the option to leave just had not presented itself yet.

Later that night, Aafree said, "Alborz you seem to be somewhere else tonight. I can see a change in you."

"No, not at all," I told her.

"Okay, let me see whether you are the same in bed."

After we had sex she said, "No I am wrong, you are the same." I succeeded that night.

She was convinced no one else was in my life. But I knew I couldn't sail in two boats at once. My choice was Pantea's boat. Anyway, I left my fate to time and to see how it would go.

The next day after we checked out, some part of the wood in the suite was burned. Of course, Herol and his friends were negligent, since they were awake until about 7 am having Sheesha. I had to pay the hotel 1,200. It was common with Aafree's sons.

I left on the evening of December 11th and came back to Mumbai on the 15th to meet Pantea. She was leaving for Iran on December 17th, 2012, to see her mom.

We stayed in the Presidential Suite at the Meridian. While having dinner at Peshawar Restaurant at the Maratha Sheraton opposite the Meridian, I told her I needed good wishes, my two five-star hotel cases had been stuck in court for several years. "I would like to give you 200,00.000 dollars for your good wishes." She said her good wishes were always with me whether I gave her anything or not.

She said, "In any case, I do not want you to give me anything. However, if you feel happy that my good wishes worked, I leave it up to you."

During our meal, she ordered Raan, a famous meat dish, but she could not eat even a quarter of the dish. Raan is a large meal, and with me being a total vegetarian, we had the leftovers packed to go. We put it in the refrigerator in our room.

Pantea was leaving in the morning, so we only had one night. The next morning, we were making love, and I was licking her pussy, but she smelled like urine. I didn't like it when women smelled bad. I advised she should wash when she urinates, and she shouted, "So, don't lick." She was very rude and hurt my feelings. We didn't have sex that morning. As usual, she was not bothered.

Pantea left for her friend's place and I started getting ready for my Delhi flight. I realized her leather jacket and Raan were still in the room. I called to let her know I would bring her things to wherever she was. She felt so guilty about her actions and leaving me unsatisfied; she showed her affection out in the open. A hug and a soft kiss felt nice.

I was thrilled by this behavior since she was soft-hearted, but being rude was her nature. It was the last time anything like that happened. She took care to make sure she was always fresh to be licked wherever.

Chapter Seven:

I Couldn't Stand It Anymore

Pantea leaving for Iran had a bigger effect on me than expected. Her lovely memories filled my every thought. I continued to see Aafree while she was gone. But by New Year's Eve, I couldn't stand it any longer. I called to hear her voice.

During the first week of January 2013, in her absence, Aafree met me with a girl named Liya. I had met her once at dinner at the JW Mumbai. As usual, we were staying in a presidential suite at the Grand Hyatt, which had two bedrooms, one room for Liya and her clients the other for us. I found the whole situation irritating.

I invited one of my officer friends Mohammad to spend time with Liya and paid Aafree. After midnight, we were alone and went off to have sex. Aafree called Liya in for a threesome, which disturbed me. Anyway, that night Aafree made Liya suck me and we didn't have sex.

Afterward, I went home; we never spent the night when in Delhi. The next day, I came to the suite and Liya took the opportunity to kiss me since Aafree was in another room. But my mind was on Pantea.

Aafree said, "I saw you, but I didn't bother you because I was distracted by other thoughts." We went to lunch.

Somehow during our visit, I got Liya's number and she got mine. The next afternoon I called to tell her we could not meet anymore. She bitched about Aafree, that they didn't go to Mumbai last evening. Instead, they went to Trident because some clients came to meet them.

I told her, "I have met someone, and do not want to be with Aafree any longer. I could use your help." She accepted.

Our deal was, I would pay 6,000 dollars to buy a car then give her 2,000 dollars a month for the next twelve months. I would tell Aafree I was in love with Liya. We agreed. It had to be this way so Pantea could be kept out of the situation since Aafree might be tempted to verbally abuse Pantea. I didn't want her to be hurt.

The next day, when Aafree reached Mumbai, I sent a text and told her I wanted to break up since I had fallen for Liya. She screamed and used dirty words, etc. Then, I found out she was not going back to Mumbai. Instead, she chose to stay in Trident. She had lied to me. I couldn't take anymore.

Liya took the brunt of her anger, as we expected. But she stayed silent since I paid her an ample amount. Three days later, I invited Liya to spend time with my officer friends. We agreed to a longer time since I was short on cash and she was getting car money in April. She had to stay quiet until the end of December of the next year.

We called Seema that night for a Mujra performance and she slept with me after the dance. The next day, when Liya left, she kissed me so passionately it caught me off guard, and I told her to leave it for some other time. It was my last evening with another girl besides Pantea, who was my life. I was waiting for her return. Pantea rested for a day when she returned, and we met in Mumbai. We spent the day together before I told her the Liya story. I left out the part about the money.

I asked Pantea, "Can we invite Rupali and Liya for drinks and dinner in our presidential suite at the Lalit Hotel?"

"Yes." Everyone agreed.

I wanted to celebrate since my days with Aafree were done, so I ordered a special cake. I was available exclusively for Pantea. The cake read, "Thanks to Liya in helping Alborz to leave Aafree."

Rupali was jealous as she was in love with me, but my heart belonged to Pantea. I had found the love of my life. I was fond of Rupali and she always told me to consider her if I left Aafree.

Later that evening, I went into the kitchen and Rupali caught me: "Salae, I was in the queue waiting for you, but it's ok you went for Pantea. She is a very good girl, and you deserve her. But why did you get help from Liya, and not me? You don't trust me; we always confided in each other." I stayed quiet.

Pantea was so good and easy. I knew she wouldn't be concerned with our conversation.

Liya cut the cake, and we had a nice evening. Pantea never expressed her feelings over me leaving Aafree, but I knew she was happy. We made love that night and her entire body was mine. She was utterly loving, so much licking for Alborz. I could be fully committed to Pantea. My life moved forward with complete happiness toward my lovely gorgeous girl Pantea, whom I wished to be fully mine one day. I did not know whether I'd be able to achieve this, as she was a different girl, and would she leave her work for me? I did not want her to lose her freedom.

Chapter Eight:

Role of Anahita

We continued to meet one to two nights a week and I thought my good time had started. Although, our plans were always at Pantea's convenience. Whatever her schedule was, I agreed. Once a month, since we both like to party, we'd invite her girlfriends and my officer friends. We met in different presidential suites around Delhi.

During our parties, some memorable events created long-lasting images. At one meeting in the Grand Hyatt suite, she told me her brother wanted to buy a car in Iran, but he needed three Lak.

"Alborz he is too young. I don't want to give him the money." Her father refused as well.

I said, "He is your younger brother, you must fulfill his wish."

Later that night after we finished partying, I started packing up the liquor, which was complimentary. She shouted, "What are you doing? Go faster! Why are you still here?"

I tried to leave, but her behavior was disturbing. Thankfully, I am patient since my love for her is strong. Pantea had a flight to Mumbai at 8 a.m. Since I lived near the airport, I was not meeting her before the flight, but texted and asked her to message when she was ready to leave.

She waited at the airport entrance for me to arrive. I handed her a sealed envelope. "What is it?" she asked.

"Nothing much," I said. Pantea was stunned to see it contained money for her brother to buy a car. She broke out in tears. "I'm so sorry for my behavior. It was unfair."

My ultimate goal was to please her in every possible way since I loved her deeply.

Valentine's Day arrived in 2013, my first year with Pantea. I arranged to have a piece of special jewelry designed. The ring had love spelled in diamonds. It had a matching bracelet and locket. I presented it at Mumbai Taj Palace

Elephanto, which is a duplex suite with a bedroom on the first floor.

I also gifted her with Sheesha and a fur pipe, which she appreciated. She presented me with wish cards, "In love, I found my truest friend, someone I can read easily, someone who is my favorite company. Ours is love so true, so pure, so complete. Holding your hand, not a moment goes by when I am not feeling delighted for having found you, for having loved you."

We had a Valentine's dinner reservation at Casablanca in the Souk Restaurant at the Taj Palace Hotel. Casablanca is a private venue for two persons. Some beautiful photos were taken by the photographer, which I presented to Pantea with love.

Pantea looked beautiful in a white dress. I could see the joy on her face. We made sweet love later that night.

She said, "Alborz... I respect you."

We stayed for two nights and parted, all paid per our agreement. Thereafter, she started trusting me and we had some great conversations.

She confessed, "I only have one Indian girlfriend named Anahita. I met her at work and she has gone to

Bihar, her home town. My Irani friends say they will take you away from me if I introduce them."

Pantea is the last love of my life. I am a steady guy, and only want her in my life. I couldn't like anyone before or after.

"Ok, I will bring Anahita to entertain your officer friends when they are meeting in Delhi."

In fact, the group consisted of Leela, Milin, her sister, Anahita, and Pantea.

In March 2013, the plan was scheduled: Milin would come first followed by Anahita. My officer friends were always looking for different girls and this arrangement suited them perfectly.

On the first night, we partied at Leela Kempensiky in the presidential suite with a separate room for Anahita. While partying on the first day, Anahita asked me many times to dance. I was reluctant because of what Pantea had said. I didn't accept. The next day Milin arrived, and we arranged a separate room as well. There was one officer and his friend, and we all partied.

Milin asked me to dance, and I accepted. After the party, I asked Milin if she had a travel ticket for the next day.

Pantea said yes, but then to my surprise, she started shouting, "Why did you ask her? Leave, please." Then she started crying.

I didn't understand what had happened. So, I asked her to make love and talk, although she did not say anything and just started crying, "Now you want to make love? Please just go home."

I realized that night, I had a place in Pantea's heart. She cried because she thought I behaved like any common man. Later, I heard that Anahita bitched about the night before when I refused to dance with her and then accepted when Milin asked.

Anahita was prejudiced against Pantea, telling her to be careful and that I liked Milin. Frankly, some girls are very bitchy and jealous.

The next day when everyone left, Pantea arrived in Mumbai. I called her. "Are you ok?"

"Yes, I am ok. But I'm not happy." I realized that Anahita was the cause of this situation.

This incident made me realize that Pantea would never reveal her heart openly, but in her heart of hearts, she wanted me to be hers exclusively. Somewhere deep down she was falling in love with me, or maybe just an attachment, as she didn't believe in love. A long-term relationship was out of the question. In fact, she made her thoughts very clear.

Chapter Nine:

I Loved Her with All My Heart and Soul

Pantea's birthday was coming in ten days on April 4th and we met at the Chandigarh JW Marriott. Of course, we were in the presidential suite. This was on March 24th.

The idea of her birthday coming and our first year together had me fascinated. So, I prepared a grand celebration and flew in an hour early to shop at Calvin Klein. Then, I found balloons that spelled out Happy Birthday Pantea.

I bought a nice flower bouquet that would welcome her to the suite. Once the room was arranged, I headed for the airport. The overzealous outpouring of my affection stunned her; she had never had anyone celebrate her birthday. It explained her limited joy on special occasions, but she let me do whatever I wished.

Earlier I had explained that my son and his five friends would come with me to Mumbai on the 4th to celebrate her birthday. I asked if she could invite Liya and Rupali. She agreed. I booked the presidential suite at the Maratha Sheraton as well as a few rooms. We invited Rupali and Liya to come with their boyfriends if they wished. My son Radin's friends made flight reservations to stay for two nights. In the suite, we had a mini-casino and arranged the best liquor brought from Delhi.

We had to arrive early to set up the casino and music system for the singer. I arranged the flowers and balloons. The arrangement was beautiful to match the girl I loved. I bought a red dress for Pantea to wear. Since she was turning thirty-five, I bought the same number of gifts to match. To enhance the experience, I hid the gifts around the room. It was like a treasure hunt. A cake was prepared, and the area was filled with family photos, plus the music she liked from Iran.

Liya arrived at three o'clock and took 6,000 dollars to buy a car, as promised by me to hide my affair with Pantea from Aafree. Pantea arrived around five so we could have some fun before the party started.

Radin's friends appreciated Pantea. "Uncle's girlfriend is hot," they told him. I agreed she was very hot, without a doubt.

When we got to the room, I gave her the dress, and she agreed to wear it for the night. Then we completed her treasure hunt and found all thirty-five gifts, however, the searching became too much for her and she got tired of looking for the last three gifts. I knew she wasn't happy with the idea but would never say anything. She graciously accepted without criticism. Innocence ran deep in her heart.

After her birthday adventure, it was time for the guests to arrive. The casino and suite were appreciated by all who attended, although some were jealous. A good-looking girl caught my attention. I'd never seen her before and we spent some time talking. Anahita bitched to Pantea. We partied until four o'clock in the morning, many of the guests were drunk and Liya was sleeping. Rupali got jealous of Liya, thinking she got to spend more time with me because of our deal. Rupali bit Liya on her shoulder unknowingly, as she was drunk and jealous. Both of them wanted me, but I was exclusively for Pantea.

Liya was so drunk her boyfriend had to take her out in a wheelchair. The guests danced and enjoyed the casino. I retired around four am, but the boys were still playing the casino games and Pantea was busy with her friends. I woke up a few hours later, and she had not come to bed. When I went to look, the boys were still busy in the casino. I found Pantea and Leela snorting cocaine. It was a birthday gift from Milin. This did not bother me; I would be able to make her leave this way of life in my own way.

We got up about 2 pm the next day and I soon found her snorting in the bathroom. It was the first thing she did when her feet hit the floor. When I told her of my displeasure, she explained it was the only way she could wake up after partying.

We planned a dinner together that evening, which she liked. Liya did not attend since she had a hangover. Rupali and many others came along. I hired a mini Mercedes bus that had an announcer's mike. However, I couldn't understand why Pantea was upset. Maybe Anahita was playing her game again. Anyway, I used the mike like a tourist guide, but nothing cheered her up.

The restaurant was busy, and even with our reservation, we had to wait. It irritated me and I was rude to the manager. Pantea was upset with my behavior. She was always a very polite person in restaurants and to hotel staff. This incident taught me a lesson, and I worked to improve my behavior, although it took some time.

After dinner, everyone wanted to go to the nightclub except Pantea. So, I suggested the Playboy Club instead. Many of the people knew Pantea since she was a party girl.

We booked a table with Gray Goose, whiskey, etc. The group partied until the club closed. As we walked out, Rupali shouted, "Mr. Azar can we take our bottles?" I told them to hurry and went to help her fetch them.

Pantea was annoyed with Rupali's behavior, but more so with me. When we reached the hotel, Rupali wanted to come up with us, but I thought under the circumstances she should leave. "I am sleepy, you need to go home." However, my actions were insulting. The next day, I explained my reasoning to Rupali. Once we got back to the room, Pantea was ferocious for my mistreating Rupali. I kept quiet.

The next day Rupali asked to have the casino packed and delivered to her house. She told me her boyfriend was fond of the entertainment. But instead, it backfired on poor Rupali. Kartil, her boyfriend, became angry with her for asking to have the casino delivered to the house.

The birthday episode left a strong message. Pantea needed my help to stop her angry streak and I needed to improve in my behavior. She told me I should behave like a gentleman, as she always said, "You are not Radin's age, you are a mature person."

We were seven months into our relationship, her first birthday with us together. I loved her with all my heart and soul. I decided to improve myself in all respects however she wanted me to.

Chapter Ten:

It's My First Birthday with Pantea

Our relationship continued to flourish the longer we saw each other. I felt the closeness, and her innocence and honesty were apparent.

My first birthday arrived with Pantea. I told her we'd celebrate on the 17th, 18th and 19th of May. Thereafter, I would be with my family. Pantea was so damn unbelievable; her understanding made me fall more in love than I could ever imagine.

I asked permission to invite an officer who could party with us one day and a different one the next. She agreed and I invited Liya. It was not their first meeting, so she felt comfortable.

As usual for my birthday, I arranged a suite at the Aman Hotel in Delhi with a private swimming pool and a singer in our room. We had a lot of fun.

My friend Mohammad enjoyed himself immensely. But, since Liya still had me on her mind, my friend was irritated. The next morning, I got up for breakfast as usual about nine-thirty. No one seemed to understand that my heart was with Pantea. I would not share myself with any other girl. Pantea was ignorant of my feelings; it did not bother her in any way. My friend joined us again the next day, and we had fun.

On the morning of my birthday, Pantea gave me an Omega watch and a sculpture of a bow and arrow saying, "Shoot at the moon; if you miss you still land in the stars". This was a perfect match for my nature. It was a beautiful choice; her thoughtfulness was overwhelming. I had figured out that even though she was tight with money, she did not mind buying gifts for me, no matter the amount. I gave her a 20Gm gold coin.

Then came the 19th, and I took the girls in a Rolls Royce Shogen IV. It's a special convertible, and there are about only six others in the world.

I asked Pantea if she wanted a picture of her with the car, but she declined. Since she'd seen everything in the world, none of this stuff mattered to her.

During the drive, my car experienced engine problems and was not running properly. So, on the way to the airport, Pantea asked why I had a vehicle like this if it did not run properly. I agreed but just wanted to give her a ride in the car. A few months later I sold the car, but my son hated me for the decision. At the time, I needed the money, so it was a good choice.

I continued to stay at the hotel with my family as it was a common ritual that I had followed all my life. We were always together on the day of my birthday. I also invited my good college friend Tita along with his family.

Chapter Eleven:

Pantea was a Beautiful Soul

Pantea continued to reduce her so-called work as our relationship developed. It was heartwarming to provide everything she needed. She was happy with me and our association bonded the love that was growing between us. It may have only been one-sided since she did not believe in love.

I remember many times she discussed how different men reacted to her work. It was shocking according to Pantea. But I knew our situation was unusual. She appreciated the love I shared with her; she never expressed any concern, although it worried her to wonder if I would ever leave and she'd be left without anything. I know she worried about putting all her eggs in one basket.

There was no question in my mind about making sure Pantea had all the comforts she could ever want. I never failed to tell her that she would never have to regret being with me.

Between May and August 2013, we met continuously about six times a month. It was all at Pantea's convenience. It was my aim to always be patient and understanding. In my mind, no amount of time was too much; my love ran deep. I do not have the words to express the passion in my heart for this woman. Pantea was my princess, my shehzadi, the queen in my life.

Our relationship developed over time, and Pantea still had anger issues, but I am a patient person and remained calm. On one occasion, I made reservations for a flight to Delhi. I called to ask if she could come one hour earlier, and she got mad. She canceled and refused to come visit.

Needless to say, I learned a lesson to never ask if the plans could be changed. Pantea does what she decides and has no flexibility in her life for anyone.

Once we met for two days at the Taj Palace in Delhi, and she had invited another new friend, Niki from Turkey. I invited my officer friends to join; one stayed the first night and the second our last night. One night we were sitting on the garden terrace listening to some good music. The suite's butler came in and he appreciated the music. (This is connected to an incident with Anahita later).

Another time we met at Leela Kempensiky with Niki again and were having a nice time. Pantea had drastically reduced her drinking, but my officer friend Mohammed insisted she drink a bottle of white wine, although she was fond of vodka. Anyway, we all were dancing in the suite; the men were wearing their underwear, and the women their panties and bras.

One of those evenings when Anahita was present, I did a lovely striptease. It started with my watch, belt, pants, specs, and finally ended with my underwear, but my friend shouted, "Alborz Azar, please stop." We all laughed, except Anahita. Thank God she didn't bitch about the incident to Pantea.

Trust me, Pantea was a good girl; in fact, there are no words to express my feelings. But she was simple, never bitchy. I don't just feel this way because of our relationship; she was actually unbelievable. However, she never liked me watching her eat. At the ITC Maurya Sheraton suite with Niki, we ordered room service, and Pantea is a foody and loves duck. I never ate much when we were together. I was watching her eat; she was fascinating, and everything she did was wonderful.

She asked, "Why are you watching me? Do you want me to eat or not?" I smiled and stopped watching.

Ajay came to Delhi on a business trip. We were staying in the Shangri-La Hotel in the presidential suite which had two bedrooms. Pantea had come with Anahita. When Ajay arrived, we went to an excellent nightclub. We got a private table and we were at the back of the room, I hinted to Ajay to take Anahita up to the room, but she found a way to complain, bitching about me to Pantea about why I was pushing them to the bedroom. Of course, later she wanted to know my reasoning, but all I wanted was for Ajay to go upstairs with Anahita. All these meetings were mostly once a month, otherwise, we were alone on other days. I always enjoyed it more when it was just us together. But Pantea seemed to enjoy partying.

Pantea had her faults, but she was never demanding or asked for anything. It's me who was always wanting something. She had a beautiful soul and would never know the depth of my love.

In the Delhi Grand Hotel, Pantea came with Leela for two days. My officer friends would come to meet with Leela on different nights. I wanted to make love before everyone arrived, but Pantea got irritated with me for taking so long.

It was her pre-period days, and she always got cranky. I realized then that she had seven pre-period days.

After we were finished Pantea went to take a bath and she yelled, "You are a kidoo."

I did not understand her meaning, which upset her as well. "You go meet your friends; I am not in the mood." I never said a word.

When my officer friend Mohammed arrived, Pantea said, "Give me ten minutes, and I'll be ready." We had a great time in the suite.

Pantea and I were dancing, and she whispered, "You have a good heart, all your works will be done." I knew it was honestly genuine. "I want to see you happy always." These words made me forget about her anger and fall deeper and deeper in love with her.

Chapter Twelve:

Our First Anniversary

I had always wanted to buy her a luxury car, but due to my financial constraints, it was not worth mentioning. However, my wish was to give it to her on our first anniversary.

One afternoon, she informed me that Leela's boyfriend was buying her a car. I asked, "What kind of car do you wish to have?"

"I've always thought about an X6 BMW." My financing was tight, but I kept that to myself for the next two years.

"I'm not asking, Alborz. You asked, so I told you what I have always wanted."

"Let's get you a car. What kind?"

"I would like a Honda CRV for the time being" she replied.

"Do you have a color preference?"

"Yes, metallic black." I agreed.

The next day without telling Pantea, I went on a treasure hunt to find a metallic black CRV. But my searching was in vain as the CRV was not made in black any longer. I did not want to tell Pantea I failed.

Since my plans had to change, I called Mr. Subhash, a friend who had a Honda agency in Bangalore. I asked him, explaining that an officer friend was looking for black only. He informed me that was not possible. "How do I get a black one?" I asked.

"You can have it painted. The original paint will be stripped. It will look like factory black."

"How long will it take?"

"Well, it's an import, so we must order and paint, about fifteen days to deliver."

"I need to have it by September 1st in Mumbai."

"I will do my best, but it may not be possible."

"Fly in the car and I will pay the extra charges."

The car was an automatic, fully loaded, but I could not fulfill my target date, our second anniversary. But that was not the only issue; the car cost 60,000 dollars. I could not pay with her bank account as she was on a student visa.

I tried to explain that she could not have the car in her name, but she insisted Leela's boyfriend had put Leela's car in her name by paying cash.

Pantea was ignorant and did not understand government laws. I explained if Leela paid cash she would have a problem later with the tax department. In fact, she did have a problem two years later. However, I wanted to do things legally so the car could be in her name. I paid for the car from my company account and had my friend create an invoice and put the insurance in her name.

On September 1st it was our first anniversary, but I failed to keep my promise of gifting her with a black CRV on our anniversary, but Pantea never said a word. I was busy with a work project, so asked her to meet in Delhi. We stayed at the ITC 1 Sheraton. I arranged for a cordless mike and wrote about my appreciation of Pantea. The devotion was about five pages long. I was reading to her in the living room and noticed how much she loved the gesture.

In her luggage, she brought a pure gold Lord Krishna and Radhe, his devotee, a true love known throughout India. I was shocked, how could she have known I believed in Lord Krishna? Pantea had a way of surprising me.

She also presented a card with the following wishes: "YOU WILL FOREVER BE MY ALWAYS... My happiness, my world, my everything. It feels like we were meant to be."

I wanted to buy her something special, so we went to the jewelry store and she picked out a ring. I always ensured that she approved, or it would never be worn.

It was my first anniversary with the only other women I truly loved besides Rozhan. My love ran deep for both women, a passion that would extend beyond life itself.

I kept telling Pantea that the car was being shipped in brown, but it would be stripped and painted in the black metallic color, as per her liking. However, the car would not arrive in Mumbai until the end of September, despite my best efforts.

The car arrived in black and a friend's driver drove it from Bangalore to Mumbai on October 13th. Pantea did not know the car was being delivered. I wanted it to be a surprise.

We were staying at the Hyatt Regency. She asked me to order some cocaine. I agreed. The dealer came to the corner, and we exchanged money. It was fifty dollars, Pantea was worried about me making the exchange and watched from the hotel room. I was not worried and would never do anything to put her in harm's way. She was so impressed.

My surprise was coming later. I recommended the Martha Sheraton Pan Asian Restaurant for dinner. I suggested we walk because I knew the car was coming. The driver was coordinating the delivery via text. I had to make several excuses to use the restroom, and Pantea wondered what I was doing. The car arrived, and I met the driver outside the hotel, got the keys, and let him go.

We left the restaurant. "Let's go in this car," I said and tossed her the keys; she was stunned.

We sat in the car looking over the interior. When she saw the automatic gears, she was reluctant to drive. "You drive; I have never driven automatic."

"Okay," I replied.

We drove to an empty lot so she could practice. I know it was more exciting to me than Pantea, but I loved it. It was my first success with her, and she repaid with a passionate kiss. "I love you."

She drove the car back to the hotel, and we made love. It was an incredible evening. The next morning, I told her to get the car washed, since it had come from Bangalore and was dirty. We got up late and ate breakfast in the room. I explained, "After I iron my clothes, we can get the car washed."

"No, you go. I will iron the clothes." Pantea hated ironing.

Once we finished all the chores, we made love and went out for the evening. She drove to the Four Seasons hotel to have dinner. Pantea wanted to pay, but I would never let her pay for anything. Besides, she was my love beyond anyone else in my life, except for my wife Rozhan.

We parted ways the next day; she was very excited to drive her new car. I was just happy to see the joy on her face.

Chapter Thirteen:

She Sang the Song Tu Mera Hero (You Are My Hero)

The purchase of Pantea's car took some time to sort out. My finances were tight, so I had to borrow money for the CRV. But it was a special gift, and I wanted to fulfill her wish.

Once we got to the registration process, the invoice was in her name, although my company paid the bill. This was all thanks to my friend Mr. Subhash, who made my wish come true.

Fate was on my side: there were no objections about the document or the order, so once I engaged with an agent from the transport authority at Andheri West the issue fell upon the top officer. Mr. Shindley was a hard nut to crack. He refused to register the car in her name since she was a foreigner on a tourist visa.

This challenge was another test for me to overcome. We also faced difficulties in getting police verification. But Pantea would never agree to go to the police station.

However, I called Parmani, the property dealer who got us the flat. I explained the issue and I convinced her to come along with me to the police station. She signed the form on Pantea's behalf and put her thumbprint on the documents. I was so impressed by her help; she agreed to complete the process with me, as I was the landlord of the flat.

Parmani convinced the police, along with giving them some money, and explained that since the landlord was present, there should be no problem. Thank God it was done.

Once the police verification was completed, it was time for Pantea to sign. I contacted her and asked if I could come to her home for the signatures; she agreed. But when she saw the papers, she wondered if she would need permission to sell the car if necessary, and she started crying.

Pantea was completely ignorant about such instances and misunderstood my intentions. I explained that she would not need my signature. After some discussion, she signed. The paperwork was submitted to the transport authority, but Mr. Shindley refused to sign off. The next business day, I made an appointment to convince him to agree. He was adamant about meeting with her in person in his office.

I knew getting Pantea to meet with Mr. Shindley would be very difficult. He explained there have been many incorrect cases of cars being registered to foreigners. But, being a very honest man, told me he would not sign off on the papers. He demanded to meet with Pantea alone. It was the only way to get the car registered in her name. I explained that as her guardian I would come along, but he insisted it had to be her alone.

Our discussion continued about her being a young foreign girl, but he assured me she would be treated respectfully. I did not see why he had to speak with her alone.

"Is her flat nearby? Call her now," he said.

"She is not feeling well today, that's why I came alone."

"I must see her in one or two days, okay?"

I agreed, and he gave me his visiting card with the mobile number to call. When I got back to Delhi, I had to call to confirm the day Pantea would meet with him. The option gave me no choice but to convince her to meet with him.

I explained to her repeatedly that it was the only way to get the car in her name even though the police verification was done. Needless to say, the tension was high for several hours. Pantea finally called her girlfriends and discussed the situation on the phone with them for hours. Once her call was over, she agreed to meet with Mr. Shindley.

We discussed what their conversation would entail. The whole scenario was stressful. But, over the next few days, I got her ready for the appointment.

We went to the hotel from the apartment in her car, and she kept asking why she had to go meet him. I waited in the lobby while she met with Mr. Shindley. He very respectfully asked her to sit on the sofa and wait while he pulled the file. Pantea explained she was living in my uncle's apartment. Then she gave him her permanent address. She went on to explain that she attended Poona University five days a week for her studies.

Pantea's sophistication made speaking with her easy. Mr. Shindley wanted to see her driver's license and explained it was a heavy vehicle license. He immediately cleared her car registration and directed her to the correct license on the application. He also advised if she had any further issues to contact him directly. It was an exhilarating experience for Pantea; she accomplished something important with my help. Her trust in me was developing quickly.

We went back to the hotel, and she expressed her appreciation. It was nice to hear her apology for doubting my ability to succeed in this endeavor. For me, it was true love, and although I knew Pantea's feelings were different, I was winning her over slowly.

It took some time but her call girl work was cut by more than ninety-five percent. I didn't want to remain her Chipkoo, as she had saved me in her phone. My intentions were to be her hero.

During the first week of September 2012, she was dancing to the song "Tu mera hero, subha honay na dey tu mera hero" (You are my hero let not the sun rise) and pointing at me.

Chapter Fourteen:

One Day She Would Fall in Love with Me

Pantea shared some of the best news I had ever heard. Anahita was getting engaged and would be married soon and was going to settle down in London. "Alborz... I will miss her."

Pantea had some comments about Anahita and her fiancé. They were supposed to get married in December 2014. She explained that one evening during a conversation, Anahita was drunk and said "Darling I'm drunk" and talked to her fiancé on the phone. His concern was over how she was behaving. When she was planning the wedding, Pantea was upset because Anahita did not offer to buy her a plane ticket to come to her wedding in Goa. I asked why she was upset. Pantea was here with me, and I could buy her the ticket.

One meeting we were at Claridge's Hotel in Delhi and we went to a Spanish restaurant for dinner and Pantea went to the washroom after we came back to the room. I always followed her wherever she went, and I realized she was a bulimic (purging after a meal).

Pantea got very upset with me and asked, "Why do you have to follow me everywhere?" I know she was embarrassed. Thereafter, I never followed her again.

I purchased Pantea a club card at the JW Marriott in July 2013. She liked to swim and use the gym sometimes. Christmas was coming, and I wanted us to spend part of the holiday together. I reluctantly asked if she'd spend two nights with me in Mumbai. We planned to meet on December 23, 2013, at the Marriott. I messaged and asked her to bring the vouchers for the club card. In fact, I needed the stay vouchers to get a discount on the room.

In my failure to explain, she was hurt by my words, "All the vouchers."

We were having dinner, and she was talking about how much she would like some cocaine. I agreed to get her 5 grams for 250 dollars. It was the same routine as last time: meet outside the hotel and bring the cash. She said she wanted me to buy 1kg, and being that I am good at calculations, I figured that would cost 60,000 dollars, as much as the CRV.

I may have repeated the same thing a few times, and it apparently hurt her feelings once again.

We went back to the room, and she threw the vouchers on the table, saying "Here are all club vouchers, I don't need any of them."

The incident surprised me; I had to explain that I just wanted the stay vouchers. She was hurt twice by my statements. We shouted at each other. I threw the vouchers away, and she walked out of the room. A few minutes later, I sent her several messages but it was all in vain. It was our first fight in fifteen months. It was terrible; I had paid for two days and my flight was not until the 25th. I kept calling until the next morning, but she was very angry. Her stubbornness showed clearly. She had told me many times how she forgot her other boyfriends for one time incidents; this was a serious situation.

I left on the 24th one day earlier than planned. I continued to pacify her through various messages, but to no avail. I would be the only one to repent. After twenty-three days, she agreed to meet me in Delhi to discuss the situation.

We had lunch at Oberoi's Gurgaon, although the conversation was one-sided. I had no idea what her plans entailed. Would she break up with me or continue as a couple?

We went back to the room and she started complaining about the situation. I listened patiently. If my actions were not completely calm, she would break up with me.

The words she said were hard to hear: "Aafree wasted her life for you since the relationship didn't last longer than thirteen years. She lost her youth, otherwise, Aafree could have gotten married."

I very politely explained she was divorced with two sons. "I didn't spoil her youth; it was a mutual relationship. Besides, she benefited very well from the situation. I bought her a bungalow, a car, etc."

"Since we met, I have reduced my work by eighty percent over the last fifteen months. I don't even answer the calls when they come through."

I understood her point; she had started depending on me. Pantea was insecure and concerned I might walk away. I politely explained that would never happen; she could depend on me and our relationship. We made love, and the fight ended. It was a difficult situation, but our bond strengthened. One day she would leave her work and rely on me without any doubts. It was very difficult, almost impossible, to be in love, as she always believed love was for youngsters and we were too old for that kind of stuff. Besides, she never believed in love, she always wanted her space and freedom, and she would never ever claim her rights to a man.

Chapter Fifteen:

You Didn't Have to Do So Much

Life was moving forward, and Pantea and I were growing closer every meeting. At the end of January 2014, her parents were coming to visit. Her parents had been informed that her studies were done and that she was working. This caused concern, and she asked me if I could prepare some files. Pantea told her father she was working as a dietitian consultant.

I started working on the documents immediately. My staff arranged about twelve files to show an active client list. The paperwork looked great.

We arranged to meet in Mumbai, but when I presented her with the documents, instead of showing appreciation she shouted, "You didn't have to do so much."

Then she reduced the files to four. Needless to say, her actions left me altered. Later after she thought about her what she had done, she felt bad and appreciated my hard work. Although she'd never ever apologized. I accepted her character; I knew it very well.

She asked me to book a room in Goa for her and her parents. I made the reservations immediately. Pantea bought the plane tickets by herself, but I think it bothered her that I didn't offer to pay. Thereafter, I understood such things and she would always pay me back by adjusting my dues.

The visit with her parents lasted about two weeks, and the time apart was difficult. I missed her. However, several times she offered to sneak away and give me a few hours.

Pantea's mother stayed until the end of February, but we were able to meet for a few hours on Valentine's Day 2014, I arranged a romantic evening. My gift was an Italian gold ring. She loved it.

She brought gifts for me and a card that said "NEXT TO YOU. We share kisses and promises, plans and hopes, D=dreams and decisions, milestones and memories. WE LOST OUR HEARTS IN NO TIME. And it felt so easy… Just like magic… Love is you and me together forever."

Later that year, we had an amorous evening at Agra and visited the Taj Mahal. It is one of the Seven Wonders of the World. We stayed at the Oberoi Vilas. Our dinner was served on the terrace and the scenery was magnificent (yes, the Taj Mahal as well). It was a full moon, so the light glowed white behind the historical site.

Pantea called Leela and told her about our romantic evening. My plans worked; she loved the experience. Afterward, she took some nice pictures. I loved it when she saved them on her phone, plus it was nice being able to look at them when we are apart.

Our relationship moved to a new level; it was not just about sex or buying things to make Pantea happy. One time, during our stay at the JW Marriott at Hyderabad, I asked if she would play flash with me - a three-deck card game. We played for several hours, but I didn't want her to lose. I made sure she won the game finally, including letting her cheat. It was fun watching her enjoy the time we spent together.

It was my goal to show Pantea that I did things out of love. It was about giving, even though she didn't believe in love. I was sure that one day, she'd leave her work behind and love only me. Maybe, she would even say "I love you."

Pantea introduced me to Nowruz, Persian New Year. It is celebrated worldwide by various ethnolinguistic groups. They rejoice on March 19, 20, or 21. The holiday is also called: Novruzit (Albanian), Novruz, نوروز Новруз (Azerbaijani), Наүруз, Nawruz (Bashkir).

The holiday was on March 19th that year. I asked Pantea to be home, as someone would be delivering a package. She needed to bring it the next time we met. The envelope contained 2,000 dollars. Pantea appreciated having someone in her life that truly cared for her well-being.

Anahita left for London in March to move in with her husband. It was a time of rejoicing for me. One day I was at the Hyatt China Kitchen restaurant in Delhi with an officer. I left at around 10:30 pm and sent a message to Pantea. I always loved to hear her voice, but only called when she told me it was okay. When I finally spoke with her, she seemed nervous and was crying. I asked what happened.

"Should I come to Mumbai?"

"No, it's okay," she replied.

"What's wrong then?"

"I had an accident with the car…" She waited for me to yell. "All the airbags burst on the front side. Leela was with me sitting in front; I was driving and reached to change the music. I didn't see the divider."

"It's okay, as long as you both are safe. No one was sleeping on the roadside and died. What's there to cry about? Everyone is safe and the car can be fixed."

She had the car towed and parked near her apartment. It had happened a few days prior, but she was afraid to tell me. Pantea was so innocent, she didn't even know how to handle the situation. I flew in the next day and took care of the repairs. I had to make three trips to get the CRV to the Honda repair facility to be fixed. When the insurance claim was filed, I informed them it was me driving, but they would not cover one hundred percent of the bill. I had to pay forty percent since it was not comprehensive insurance. I agreed.

A few days later the estimate was completed. It would take twenty-five to thirty days. Since the car was an import the parts were hard to find. It was a large list of repairs: the front side is completely gone, suspension, airbags, driveshaft etc.

We met the evening after the car was delivered for repair, and she was like a little child. Pantea has a good heart and I never wanted her to change. I all=ways worked hard and put all my effort into building her confidence in me.

Chapter Sixteen:

Incident of Gunshots

Pantea's car was still being repaired on her second birthday with me. Our time together went by too fast. While her car was being fixed, I offered a hired car several times, but she refused most of the time.

For her pre-birthday celebrations a car picked her up, and we were supposed me meet at the Intercontinental Hotel on Marine Drive. I finally decided to tell her about my arrest in April 1995 in Delhi when I was brought to Colaba down this road. I told her incidentally the FIR was registered on the 4th of April, her birthday, and was closed on September 1, 1998, when we met. The police had me in custody for fifteen days on a frivolous charge. I was made a scapegoat by the government. My financial situation was completely finished; otherwise, I would have been worth 2,000,000,000 dollars. As I explained what happened, it reminded me of an occurrence with a reporter named Miss.

Shivangi who had flown on the same flight. The case was registered by a superintendent who was fond of being in front of the cameras. He loved the limelight and wanted to be in the newspapers and magazines.

We landed at midnight in Mumbai. The airport was full of reporters since the case was prominent in the media. Plus, my business rivals' purpose was to ruin my reputation and destroy me financially.

Mr. Y.G. Singhla was a media-hungry man and wanted to destroy my company. A complete account of this story will be in another book for those readers who are interested.

I cannot forgive Y.G. Singhla for such nasty and hurtful words; his actions are unpardonable. They were the selfish actions of a desperate man. I explained to Pantea my hotel chain dream has been fucked up in bureaucratic red tape because of one man's hateful actions.

Y.G. Singhla told his DSP, who was otherwise a drunkard, "I have reduced Mr. Azar's dream five-star hotel chain to zero, his passions have been demolished." His DSP died two years later due to his poor habits.

Due to the holiday Good Friday, I was not able to get bail. Then came Saturday and Sunday, and before long a week had passed. On the following Monday, the judge who agreed to set bail was injured and took a leave for two days. Then, the ex-Prime Minister at the time of the country died, and as a result, two holidays were declared. Ambedkar's Day, a national holiday, followed and then it was the weekend again. So, fourteen days passed. Every day I was taken to the police station to bathe and change my clothes. Mr. Y.G. Singhla told me he was going to destroy the biggest industrialist in the case of oil fields bribery. However, as they became aware of the situation he was transferred.

Singhla was later shunted, and he became a lawyer of no repute. He was exposed on Wikipedia due to being a media-hungry man. I was also reported on Wikipedia because of a case blown open by the media, although the accusations were totally false and without merit. The frivolous case was finally closed after three years, but I was ruined financially and otherwise. A detailed account will be given in another book.

I explained my history to Pantea because we were going to stay at the Intercontinental Hotel, where I had stayed for fifteen days from May 1st, 1995. But, at that time it was called the Natraj Hotel. I was forced to stay in Mumbai during this time because of the bail conditions. However, I saw a different girl secretly each night.

Interestingly enough, Pantea had heard about the scandal, but she was of the view that I was a good man and was sure I had been wronged.

I asked Pantea the next day on her birthday what gifts she wanted for her birthday.

She would never tell me or say anything. "Maybe a watch?" I asked.

"A Rolex?" she replied.

We went to the Rolex showroom. Pantea picked out the one she wanted. The dealer agreed to take 10,500 dollars but I was stuck on 10,000 dollars. We walked out and I knew she wanted that one. "I will give you 500 dollars,"

"Let's go," I stated. The watch was beautiful and she was happy.

That evening I planned an exclusive pool party for her birthday, but it was only the two of us. She looked stunning as always, wearing a turquoise blue dress with the Rolex. I took some photos that we saved, and Pantea looked like a queen.

But the party's location reminded me of an incident that happened on November 26th, some years prior. Several people were killed by some terrorists in the Taj Mahal Palace Hotel. You could see the fire burning from our present location. For some reason, that year I was not able to book accommodations at the Taj Hotel and ended up staying at the Intercontinental. After dinner, I decided to take a walk down the street and take a closer look during the incident. The gunshots could be heard all over the area.

Pantea was stunned to think I was so daring. "I would never have walked out to see what was happening."

We parted as usual after two days, but I always paid her for each day per our agreement.

Chapter Seventeen:

She May Stay at My Side

While Pantea's car was being repaired, I kept following up on the status. I sent a message and arranged to meet in Mumbai. I wanted to meet her around 2 pm but she shouted, "Why? I have a nail and spa appointment. I can meet you at the Taj Hotel later when I am done."

Pantea was upset when I insisted, we meet at her home, and that she could go to her appointment afterward. But she reluctantly agreed.

I landed at 11 am but told Pantea I was arriving at 1 pm. It gave me time to pick up her car. My hired car negotiated the route since I was unfamiliar with the roads. It was 2 pm sharp when I arrived. "Why did you want to meet here?"

"I just wanted to see you at home since I was missing you." She was very confused since I never insisted, we meet at her flat.

"Oh… here is your car key." I handed the key over when I left her apartment.

My surprise was well-received; she was speechless. I got a kiss and loved to see her smile. "I will see you at the hotel after your appointment." I proceeded to the hired car.

A few minutes later, she called. "Thank you." I could hear the emotion in her words. It was from the heart.

My birthday arrived on May 19, 2014. As usual, we stayed together for two days prior and then I spent the next few days with my family. We stayed at the Claridge's Faridabad, the presidential suite with two bedrooms.

I asked her to bring Leela for one day and Milin on the second night. Seema and another dancer came to perform for two days. Seema told me she knew Milin; she used to perform the same dances.

Later that night, I informed Pantea, but she got angry and started shouting at Milin. She was yelling at Milin for half an hour. It made me feel guilty for saying anything.

The next morning when Milin left, I went to see her off at the hotel porch and apologize. "It's okay, Alborz. It happens."

After returning, I went to Seema's room to discuss it with her and explain. She told me I misunderstood the situation. She only meant they were into the same performances.

The explanation did not make me feel better; I had to find a solution. So, I made Pantea sit down and let me explain my mistake, and finally, she understood. Leela came to meet my friend Mohammad who was coming in the evening to stay with her. Seema and her friend performed. While we were dancing, Pantea and Leela went to their room. They were gone for about an hour, disgusted and thinking we men were flirts. But I swear it wasn't me. Although, I must admit to having sex with Seema earlier. Needless to say, it was a pointless gesture since my heart belonged to Pantea.

Pantea appreciated hearing the truth about what had happened the night before since I explained it was my mistake, not Milin's. Pantea had really started to like being in a relationship with me, but telling her to the truth was a mistake.

> In the past when I would say, "I like you."
>
> She would respond, "Like."
>
> Then I'd reply, "No... I love you."

Her expression showed me love was hard for her to fathom, but deep down she wanted to love me back. On occasion, Pantea would tell me she loved me.

Our second anniversary was on September 1st and we headed for the Taj Faluknama, the same place we met in 2012. We spent two nights there. By this time, the bond between us was growing very strong.

She presented me with gifts, one of which was a Sabrosky horse, a wish that I should win my property case.

The card he presented had the following written inside:

"Meri Jaan (you are my life). It's time for you to live up to your success, smile and take a bow. Congratulations!! The little joys that become beautiful memories, the many tears that my heart can hold, you are the most precious gift of them all…WHERE YOU ARE IS WHERE MY WORLD IS. You are the music of my heart… My soul's rhythm, you are the best part of my life," Meri Jaan.

The month was growing more stressful by the day. Pantea's visa was expiring at the end of September. It was very tiresome to worry about the outcome. The option to renew the student visa was off the table.

I came up with the option of applying for a business visa, as an employment visa was not possible. I met with some officers and discussed the choice, but they sent me to the FRRO office. I was informed that the only option for a business visa was from Iran. Thereafter, they could help. Once the Board of Directors meeting was over and I got their approval in appointing her as an independent director, we prepped the papers.

A short time later, an issue arose in Chandigarh that had to be settled. I contacted Pantea and asked if she would come so we could get the paperwork for the visa finalized. She agreed.

I finished my business at about 5 pm and Pantea had arrived earlier in the afternoon. The situation was demanding and I was struggling to get the issue resolved. Pantea could sense my concern and asked me to lie down in her lap. It was the first time I felt her actions came from the heart. She ran her hands through my hair so lovingly.

After I relaxed, we discussed the paperwork for the visa. Afterward, we had a drink; as usual, I had a beer and Pantea drank a glass of white wine. She had stopped drinking vodka.

There was no reason to drink and forget what she was doing for work.

"With you, I don't feel the need to drink unless we party. I like this relationship with you."

I was so impressed by the development of her emotional maturity. Pantea had left her work completely by now. The love of my life was falling in love with me. My wishes were coming true.

The only major concern was getting her visa renewed. I had a few days to get the visa renewal issued. Pantea was leaving for Iran in a few days. My goal was a five-year business visa. I could not let this lovely woman leave my side.

Chapter Eighteen:

I went to Iran

When Anahita left for London, I was happy. She was a typical girl from Bihar. Pantea was swayed by whatever Anahita said. She had a way of playing with her mind. Although Pantea was well balanced and could make her own decisions, it still had an effect.

Pantea was preparing to leave for Tehran to get her visa renewed. We had completed her paperwork, and I gave her the application for a business visa. I even signed the blank papers, so that if she had to write anything else and submit it from the company's side, it could be done easily.

I also contacted a friend of a friend in the government and scheduled an appointment with the second in command at the Indian Embassy in Tehran. Pantea was not aware of my plans since she would get mad if I insisted on coming along. My flight was on October 1st. She planned to leave on the 4th. I arranged for a visa for myself; it was a difficult task, but at the last minute she changed her flight to leave on the same day. It left me no choice but to inform her of my arrangements. To my surprise, she was glad to have me come along.

Pantea arrived in Tehran before my flight. I have traveled all over the world, but it was my first trip to Iran. At the airport, I grabbed a taxi driver who spoke some English. I was grateful. We made plans for him to remain in my service until I finished my work at the Embassy.

In Iran, Pantea and I could not stay together, so we met outside the Embassy gate. She was staying at her aunt's house, and I was at a hotel. When we went to our appointment, she stayed in the waiting area. I met with the government official and explained I wanted to develop business in Iran and had appointed this girl as a director of my company. I showed him all the documents and gifted him with a gold coin as a goodwill gesture, although he was reluctant to accept. I invited him for dinner but he declined. Pantea waited patiently in the lobby, but her nerves were on fire. After my meeting with the second man in command, who was helpful, a call was placed for an appointment with the consulate. The man at the consulate was very tough. All my hopes for success were being shattered. We were applying for an employment visa, not a business visa he stated, which was not possible.

I tried to convince him it was for exports but to no avail. I went back to Mr. Sangria, the second man in command at the Embassy and explained. I was informed of his negativity. He suggested, a few weeks prior, there had been a high official meeting about the Rice Association. Anyone who is associated with the Rice Association would be granted a visa. Mr. Sangria called and scheduled an appointment, but advised we may need a letter from the Chamber of Commerce.

I came down and explained the situation to Pantea. We would go tomorrow and get a letter of recommendation, plus we might need a letter from the Chamber of Commerce. Pantea said that her brother knew some people that might be able to help, but she could not disclose that I was with her in Iran.

It took some talking to convince her we would not fail. She went home, and I went to the hotel. I spent the entire night emailing companies and requesting letters, but in the end, it was a failure. No one responded. I was not willing to accept leaving Iran without my love.

My taxi driver Hamid was a nice guy, and I asked him for a beer. It was a dry country so no liquor was allowed. He informed me he could get some homemade fruit beer. I agreed and gave him money. Several hours later, he arrived. It was almost 11 pm. To my surprise, it was not fermented and very sweet, however, my options were limited and I had no choice. The beer had a good kick; I drank two bottles, but then it made me hungry. Down in the lobby of the hotel, there was an Italian restaurant. I had a full-size pizza. It was delicious, way too good. I was totally impressed by Iran.

The next day, I asked Hamid to take me somewhere to exchange money. I got about two thousand Euros. It was a lot of currency for Iran since everything was very cheap. To keep it safe, I left it in the money box in the cab. We went to the mall for lunch, but Hamid would not sit with me since he was just the taxi driver. I tried persuading him but to no avail. So, we went to a fast-food restaurant instead. He helped me with my order and then left. I was worried that if he took off, my money would be gone. After some time, I checked the parking lot, and he was still there. I felt comfortable. In fact, he was a very honest man.

Pantea and I arranged to meet the next day in the hotel lobby. We rode in the same taxi. She and the driver were speaking Persian and I did not understand. He was very talkative. I had already explained she was my business director and we had come to get her visa renewed.

The Chairman of the Rice Association was very kind. We got some dried fruits and Persian sweets to eat. Pantea translated while he dictated the letter to his secretary. A few minutes later, the letter arrived. It was signed and recommended Pantea for a visa. We proceeded to the Embassy but Mr. Sangria was not available. He had been called away for the afternoon, although he was kind enough to take my call and I read him the letter aloud. The letter had to be adjusted for multiple entries, he advised.

I reluctantly explained to Pantea because she would complain. However, I was able to convince her to come along to see the Chairman of the Rice Association. He was very receptive. When we arrived and explained, he promised to have it in an hour. It would be waiting at the reception desk with the changes and a multiple entry business visa. We went back to the Embassy, and I went up to meet Mr. Sangria. But, in the meantime, while I was upstairs, Pantea was downstairs, and a junior officer asked why she was waiting. Pantea, being an innocent soul, explained. In the next few minutes, the officer had her in tears, telling her it was impossible to get a visa.

Mr. Sangria advised me to apply the next day, and he would speak to Mr. Nanda at the consulate. I was quite happy with the progress until I found Pantea was in tears again. I consoled her and she calmed down but was convinced it would not happen.

We went back to the hotel and had a late lunch. Our talk lasted a long time, and she stated the only way was to get an ex visa. "Will you marry me?" she asked.

"Of course, but let's see what happens."

The discussion made her relax somewhat; she was concerned about having to stay in Iran. According to her, the only solution was a proposal of marriage. However, it would only be to get her visa, otherwise, it was against her principles. I sent her a message. "You're going to be my wifey."

"Shut up," she said, her usual loving response.

Under duress, she applied for the business visa the next day. I kept calling Mr. Sangria and pushing the issue. As I was about to board my plane, the phone rang. It was Mr.

Sangria stating that her visa was approved and she could come the next day to pick it up. It was a turning point in my life. I was happy to have succeeded in my quest.

I immediately called Pantea but was disgusted there was no answer. I sent several messages, and a few minutes later she called. I gave her the good news, but she thought it was a joke. She had just landed in Tabriz and would have to wait for four days since there were two official holidays in between. Then, she remembered her photo that was pasted to the application was without a scarf on her head. I made one more urgent call to Mr. Sangria. The verification was approved and it would not be a problem that the visa contained a photograph without a scarf. Pantea was so innocent; it's what made me fall in love with her. I was content for my flight to Delhi. We prevailed against all odds. Pantea still wanted to apply for her ex visa. She was not convinced everything would be alright. So, I inquired about the law and found it was not possible to marry even just for her visa. It would lead to bigamy.

I called her to explain, but she said, "Find me a dumb boy so I can get a spousal visa."

Pantea went back in four days and got her visa. She was so happy; the business visa was for six months and had multiple entries. She sent me a picture of the visa, and it had a maximum of a thirty-day conditional stay. We talked and she cried again.

I immediately made several inquiries with known sources. I was told to get a condition deleted from the home ministry of the country. She made a trip to Delhi and got the registration with FRRO, as it was compulsory. She applied for the removal of the condition. It was really demanding, but I never felt pressured over the situation. I was doing this for my Pantea, whom I love as much as my wife Rozhan.

I pursued all my sources to get the visa's condition removed. On the twenty-ninth day, I arranged for a Sri Lanka and Dubai visa if the condition was not removed in 30 days. She had to go to another country for a day and come back for 30 days to satisfy the condition. Pantea was very tense over the incident, but now she was safe for the next five months. She called me her hero. She changed my name to number 1hero and number 2 hero in her phone contact list.

Chapter Nineteen:

My Reluctance Showed Clearly

Perseverance made me victorious, and I won over Pantea. When I'd say, "I like you," she'd pucker her face and really wanted me to say, "I love you." Slowly, over time she started to say I love you in return sometimes. The gesture brought joy to my life.

I'd waited patiently for the time when she would leave her work forever although she was not the kind to be mine. In my heart, I knew the transition would be difficult for Pantea to accomplish. One evening I went to the washroom, and as I walked past, "Ashoka is here, are you free?" showed up as a text on her phone. Then, after I left the restroom her message alert sounded and I could read the text. I knew Pantea was not bothered by not meeting anyone else since she was only relying on me. I'd finally won her heart.

Pantea was an innocent girl with a good heart. She disliked drama and didn't lie. She was one in a billion, like my wife

Rozhan. My life had become exciting; my feelings were beyond words.

Our relationship moved to being seen together in public. She would finally walk with me through the hotel lobby, or anywhere except nightclubs. Pantea was shy that way. But soon Anahita would be returning from London for good, and I knew the situation would make my life unbearable.

Anahita would bitch in her own simple way, but Pantea was happy to see her return. So, I had to be joyful as well. Although she was a very good friend to my girl, Anahita played games with her mind. But I had no choice; the outcome was left to destiny. I was in Pantea's heart after all this time we spent together.

The next time we met, I had a delicate subject to discuss and my reluctance showed clearly. My finances were tight, and I needed to sell the flat where Pantea was living. It was a relief when she agreed without an argument. We started looking for apartments to rent, but she did not like the ones I found. Although, she knew of a Berprings apartment. I was comfortable with her choice; they were good places. Pantea suggested we use the same dealer as in the past, only these Berprings were in different areas. The only available units were four bedrooms, but she did not want more than two bedrooms. I loved her sensibility.

Padma showed us another unit at Berprings, and we agreed it was the right place. Our agreement came to 1600 dollars with an increase of 10 percent the following year. The contract took about a week to draft but it could take longer if that person is a foreigner.

I agreed to execute a company lease, and Pantea was directed to be the only tenant as director of the company. It was all agreed and done on November 19th, 2014. The flat where she was living went up for sale. I lost a bit of money selling it, but these things are expected. The new flat and Anahita coming back meant a fresh start in our relationship.

After we got Pantea's things moved, she wanted to buy a dining room table. She took me to a shop and we found one; it was scheduled to be delivered at 6 pm but did not arrive until around 9. It was the first time in more than two years I spent time in her apartment. We made love for the first time on her bed while we waited. It was her idea since she knew I was getting bored. She had a lovely collection of teddy bears. I stayed on my best behavior since it was the first to spend time in her flat.

I wanted a beer, but she could not find the opener. I noticed the neighbor's door was open and asked if I could ask them for an opener. She agreed. I got the opener and promised to return it within an hour. But upon delivery of the table, we noticed damage to the top portion. Pantea was upset. We decided to speak with the furniture store and have another one delivered. As usual, she was impressed that I could handle any situation that came into her life.

Once the situation was resolved, we decided to have dinner at the JW Marriott Juhu, where I was staying. I returned the bottle opener, and we proceeded to the elevator. A young guy came out of a neighboring apartment.

He asked if we were new neighbors. "Yes," I replied.

When we got out of the elevator and into her car, she started shouting, "Why did you reply to him? I am the one who lives there, not you. Just because you are paying rent doesn't mean you live with me." Her words were never-ending. "You did not have to say 'we', rather yes she is a new neighbor."

I wanted to say something; the outburst hurt my feelings. Although, if I lashed out it would be me coming back to apologize.

It took serious control to remain quiet. I wanted to tell her to stop the car and let me out. I'd get my bag and go home. But my love kept me silent. When we finally reached the hotel, she felt guilty as usual and apologized. Once her lips kissed mine all was forgiven. The incident left a lasting impression on my heart because she insulted me for no reason. However, it was serious, as she didn't want the neighbors seeing men coming in and out of her apartment.

Chapter Twenty:

Entry to Her Home Not Welcome

Our year ended with Christmas on my mind. Since we had fought the previous year, I did not want to spend another holiday arguing. So, to avoid the subject, I kept quiet and waited for Pantea to make a suggestion. A few weeks before Christmas, she made the decision to stay with me in Delhi. We decided to have dinner at the Westview restaurant. As always, she looked gorgeous. As a matter of fact, she had become an asset to my family. Pantea was magnificent in every aspect.

Christmas of 2014 was a beautiful holiday. In January we went to Dubai since she had a multiple entry business visa valid until April 2015. We went abroad; she was crazy for shopping. It was amazing: Pantea would leave at ten in the morning and come back after seven in the evening. The only reason she returned so early was because she felt guilty leaving me alone.

I admit her shopping was practical. She never failed to bring me something, plus her taste was very classy. We had dinner one evening at the local Iranian restaurant. Pantea always ordered cholae kabab, her favorite. It was one thing she missed from home.

From the moment we met, Pantea stole my heart. I always felt good in her company. Nonetheless, after our stay in Dubai, we were waiting at the airport and I noticed her on the phone with someone. Until that day, she had stopped talking privately so the conversation caught my attention. I noticed a glow in her eyes; she was laughing, talking freely with the person. A noxious pit grew in my stomach. Something was wrong; Pantea was in love with someone else.

The thought hurt deep inside, but I kept silent. I would forget about it later, as she was not mine exclusively; however, I wanted nothing more than for her to love me solely. I knew she never wanted to be controlled or bound to anyone, but my heart was in love. It was something I accepted. Pantea had to live her life the way she chose.

Not long after that incident, something new began. Pantea started going to the gym. It was a side of her I'd never seen. She went every morning and evening. Whenever I was in

Mumbai, she would either finish at the gym in the evening or go again first thing in the morning. Her trips lasted from 7 am to 10 am. It was suspicious when she refused to use the five-star hotel gym but instead went to the recreation center next to her house. She often informed me that she and Anahita would sit in the gym café for hours.

I had sent Pantea to an orthopedic doctor at Kokla Bhai hospital for knee pain in September the year before. She went to Dr. Shesha Jay who was a big flirt, although he already had a girlfriend, a wife, and two daughters. A love story started. He was tall, Pantea's type. She started going to the gym because he would go in the mornings at 7 am and again in the evenings after working at the hospital. Anahita was a major conspirator in the story of our relationship.

Pantea would say to her, "Alborz had done so much for me, what if he finds out?"

Anahita's response was, "You are young, Lana, and meant to have a boyfriend. Alborz is just your permanent client." Anahita convinced her she should go through with the meetings.

From then on, Dr. Jay came to her home every Saturday afternoon and left by 9:30 pm. Pantea would sometimes skip meetings with me to meet with him. At times, she would see him four to five times a week, and then would get upset with him; she was an angry bird in nature. It is important to know that I was not aware of her affair, as she always gave me the impression that she didn't believe in such things.

Besides, it was not my place to say something. As she said, "Am I married to you?"

Time flew by and Valentine's Day arrived. I booked the presidential suite at the Hyatt. Our scheduled meeting time was for 2 pm, and as usual, I arrived early. We arranged to have the hotel driver pick her up, but due to the occasion, I had some special gifts to give her so I decided to ride along.

I asked the driver to call Pantea. At that point, I went up to her apartment and reached behind my back to hand her some flowers and a teddy bear. The bear sang, "I love you." Much to my surprise, she fucked my plan. She took the flowers and bear but refused to let me come into her apartment. Then she got angry about what people would think of me coming to the door bearing gifts.

I stood outside the apartment door and waited for her, but some distance from her apartment. She played with the bear and turned to me with a smile. She handed me her bag. We went to the elevator and I knew it was going to be a bad time. We got in the car and drove to the hotel. As usual, her one-sided shouting went on for an hour. Then, she kissed me and asked me to understand. I honored her request and never went to her apartment again. The incident broke my heart; my spirit was shattered.

She opened the gifts and presented me with cards:

"It feels like bliss. Wishing your health and wealth in your life beside me. You are my koskesh valentine. Best wishes. 'Very happy valentine mera hero.' Boos Boos," Your shehzadi

"I love you... I love you ...I love you ...I love you ...I love you ...I love you ...I love you ...I love you ...I love you ...I love you ...I love you ...I love you ...I love you ...I love you ...I love you ..." (this was printed on the card)

Chapter Twenty-One:

That is Not Possible!

One time I had a business meeting with a colleague at the Four Seasons hotel. I was not able to meet Pantea in the room when she arrived. Instead, a key was sent. When I entered the room, I remember seeing a beautiful girl wearing a flashy dress with a hunter in her hand. Pantea had the opportunity to surprise me. It was a wonderful evening. The magic she brought into my life was unbelievable. Pantea did not understand love, nor the breath-taking moments it can bring to your existence.

Not long after our time at the Four Seasons, we agreed to meet in Goa. I invited my son Radin. As usual, I booked a two-room suite. My son would join us after his friends left, so he could leave when he wanted.

When I landed at the airport, Pantea was not on her flight. I messaged to find out she was sick. She had been vomiting all night and was too weak to fly. I expected to be alone all weekend, but to my surprise, she took an afternoon flight. It was very considerate; she didn't want me to be alone.

Pantea's birthday came and went. We spent the time with our usual celebrations. Shortly after, her visa was up for renewal. Thanks to a friend at the FRRO office my efforts were successful. Pantea never failed to be stunned by the industrious labor used to make her life better. In my mind, that is what happens when you love someone.

I was anxious to spend my birthday with Pantea, but something was different. She was not herself; her phone rang constantly with calls and texts. It was clear her mind was somewhere else.

However, she did bring gifts and a card that said, "The trust and friendship that we share, our happiness, that's real and rare. U+Me. You are my HONEY BUNNY. I love how you make me feel. We are in love."

When my granddaughter's birthday arrived, we arranged to meet in Goa. It was our favorite place to celebrate her birthday. I asked Pantea to invite Anahita so she would not feel lonely. It gave her time to celebrate the Goa holiday for three days. The rooms were booked at the Taj Villas, and Anahita and Pantea had their own villa. My daughter and her boyfriend had the villa next to theirs. My wife and I were below everyone else.

My family celebrated privately. We had cake, singers, and a lavish party. But it was not the same without Pantea. I missed her. I got a text asking me to save her a piece of cake, which of course, I obliged. We spent our time celebrating, but afterwards, when my two daughters were ready to leave, I asked them to give Pantea the cake. My family knew we were together, except for Rozhan; that was not possible.

Pantea was happy to have received the dessert. The next morning, we were able to meet, and I asked if she could send Anahita to the spa so we could go to her room for a few hours. Rozhan thought I was going to the spa.

I was surprised when Pantea informed me that my daughters called her a "keeper." Supposedly, when they knocked on the door and dropped off the cake, they called her my "keeper." But, deep down, the incident was upsetting, because they knew I loved Pantea and she was part of the family. In amazement, I replied, "That is not possible."

It was Anahita's bitchiness. Needless to say, I spoke with my children about the issue, and their response was what I expected. It did not happen as Pantea was told.

My daughters told me that since no one answered the door to accept the cake, they waited about ten minutes. My children knocked and said, "Housekeeping."

Anahita answered, but relayed the information to Pantea as, "Alborz's children are calling you his keep."

It was our policy that nobody says anything negative about my girl, especially my children. They knew how deeply I loved Pantea.

We met the next day at the Taj Village Chinese restaurant. Pantea and Anahita came after swimming, and Pantea was stunning as always. She asked Anahita to take our picture. The photo was lovely. In 2018, the same picture was misused by me, which has is explained in the book entitled "I DID IT." More about that story in the sequel.

Chapter Twenty-Two:

Times Were Changing

Times were changing quickly. I was called to Bangalore for a half an hour job. I called Pantea and asked if she'd like to come along. During our stay, we were sitting outside on the patio; Pantea was drinking vodka. The conversation turned to a confession about her past. In Iran, she had an affair with a boy who blackmailed her and forced her into marriage. He threatened to tell her father about their relationship. They got married due to pressure, but two days later she annulled the union as payback.

Pantea stated, "I taught him a lesson: you can't have me against my wishes."

At certain times of the month during her period cycle, she would get irritated easily and lose her temper, although I never reacted. Pantea had a stubborn streak that ran deep. Many instances she would apologize for being rude and make love to me as a pacifier.

My daughter's boyfriend Nitya was doing some kind of machinery business from Germany, and I arranged an invitation for her business visa. Pantea was convinced she'd never get the Schenegan visa due to her being an Iran national. Nonetheless, my powers of persuasion worked, and I obtained all the documents. She was granted a six-month multiple entry visa. Our trip was planned for March.

We went to Frankfurt, Milan, Monte Carlo, Paris, and Amsterdam for about twelve days. It was her first trip to Europe. Pantea was crazy about shopping. She would shop all day. I warned her one night in Milan my funds would not allow me to pay for the extra baggage. Her response was not unexpected.

She started shouting, "Just use your credit card and pay the taxes." I told her I don't use credit cards.

The situation forced me to leave the room and go for a walk. After a beer and some snacks, I went back to the room.

We tried to reconcile. "You have some issues with me, Alborz?" she asked.

I replied, "I have no issues at all, especially not with you."

I didn't realize she was guilty of something else, something that completely caught me off guard. The person on the phone was the same person each time, even when I was out for several minutes. Anyway, we talked and patched things up, we made love and moved on.

The next morning, I explained the shopping in Milan village was very good, which was a half-hour bus ride away. As usual, she was reluctant, but then she said her shopping wasn't finished in the city center, so she would come along. Pantea found a few very good stores.

We met for lunch, and she gave me a hug, "I love you. Thank you for bringing me to the village."

We traveled to Monte Carlo the next day, and I informed her we would have to dress formally and hit the casino. She was beautiful as always. Overall, she enjoyed the trip. In Paris, we went to see a famous show, Lido, and then we left for Amsterdam. Our relationship continued to progress. We grew closer each day.

During the trip, she used a sim card that allowed international roaming, which I had brought. When the cell phone bills came due, they were enormous. But I noticed a common number she called up to ten times every day. The call was to the same person she called when we were in

Dubai. I realized she was friendly with everyone and had not left her work completely; only about 99%. It could have been a close friendship with anyone.

One afternoon, I saw one of her messages pop up. "Hi, Anahita gave me your number, can we meet?"

I understood she and Anahita were sharing clients since she had not left her work completely. She gave the overflow to her friend. The situation bothered me, but I had to accept the circumstances.

When I met Pantea, she was a call girl and told me many times she would not leave her work entirely for me. Since my experience with Aafree, I understood and excepted the idea. But I was wrong, as my third book "The Aftermath of WHO DID IIT? I DID IT" will explain. Nevertheless, I was determined in my pursuit; she would leave the work one day. I knew the issues continued because of Anahita. She was very influential when it came to Pantea. Anahita played games with her mind relentlessly, to the point that she was fighting with Leela. I tried to point out the situation many times, but she refused to see the truth.

Her response was, "I am not a buccha (child), nor am I a chutiya (fool)."

One day when we were together in Mumbai, Pantea wanted to make a phone call and speak in private. She went to the corner of the room and just talked quietly. I was not bothered by the conversation and kept myself busy.

While she was talking, I went to the restroom, but then she started shouting at me when I came out. "Why are you trying to spy on me while I'm talking?"

I had no intention of eavesdropping; the fact remained that her guilt shined clear.

In August, Pantea informed me she wanted to go home to Iran. The arrangements were made and we stayed in touch. Whenever she traveled to visit home, she always came back with walnuts, almonds, and dried fruits and sometimes a very expensive rug. She knew Rozhan loved carpets. The quality was excellent and we did not have to buy them in our country. Pantea had a big heart, always unbelievable. I loved her; she was stunning in all aspects. There are no words for my love; she was an amazing woman who deserved all the pleasures in life.

Pantea finally left her work and spent all her extra time with me. I covered all of her expenses. But I felt like she needed more since she was a large part of my life. However, no matter what I did, Anahita was in the background telling her something different. We had developed a solid relationship and it made me very happy.

I understood the attachment: Anahita was one of the only people other than me to communicate with Pantea. Milin was there, but she preferred Anahita. At any rate, Anahita was not a bad person. It was just her nature to stir up trouble, especially when it came to me.

It did not help that her advice to Pantea was always, "Alborz can walk away any day from your life and you must have another person who can take care of you financially."

But Pantea was actually not a professional, she was from a very rich family and thought differently: "So what? Then I will go back to Iran."

Chapter Twenty-Three:

She Wanted Her Freedom

Our third anniversary was on September 1, 2015. As usual, we spent a full two days together, and she presented me with lovely gifts with a wish card. "Congratulations on achieving the impossible."

But the date revolved around Pantea's visa renewal. Since the previous visa was only six months, we had an early renewal date. The officer at the FRRO office, Harbhajan, was rude, and despite having all the paperwork in order, he would only approve the six months. Needless to say, I was determined to get a full year on this renewal. One of my friends is close to the external affairs minister and promised to contact the secretary of the ministry. The FRRO head agreed to an appointment. We met the same afternoon, and Pantea got her one-year renewal. However, a note was passed along to Harbhajan from his boss. Later that evening, we received a call from the FRRO office about the situation, and it made for a tense evening. When we arrived at the office the next day, it seemed the note had ruffled Harbhajan's feathers. His ego was hurt.

We were worried he would cancel her visa. However, the file was noted with an exclusion for an extensive interview to be taken of the applicant upon the next renewal. I was relieved we had a full year together, but as we left the hotel

Pantea started shouting, "You like to do the ugly (finger) everything."

Imagine my surprise. I worked intently to get her visa renewed, and instead of gratitude, she replied with anger. It was not uncommon for Pantea to lose her temper and lecture me for hours for no apparent reason. In most cases, she knew it upset me, as my face showed my discontent. But my love kept me from retaliating. I remained silent, holding onto my true feelings about the situation. Anyway, we had a year before the matter needed to be resolved again.

She had promised that if she got a visa renewal for one year, she would do karvachaut (it is a special day when a wife sees the moon and breaks the fast) with me, which in any case was very difficult for me to be away from home for. She didn't understand what it meant, although I explained it was a special day when the wife stays with her husband and fasts, which is very auspicious, and then she sees the moon and eats. Of course, she would not be able to maintain the fast, but the point was to be together that day. I committed, although I had never been away from Rozhan on this special day.

In October of that year, I planned a trip to Europe. It occurred during the particular day of my wife seeing the moon and breaking her fast. However, Pantea was unaware of this. But I always wanted to fulfill the items she expressed over the years.

We went to Portugal – Lisbon, and Cascais – and then Milan, Frankfurt village and Amsterdam village to shop, but her shopping addiction was slowing as she was a sensible girl. At times, she would buy things for me, and I always loved her choices.

Pantea planned a trip to Dubai with Anahita on November 11, 2015. I gave her a Delhi sim card to use as usual. She promised it was only for emergencies. But, when the bill arrived, the amount due was enormous: 300 dollars. Since her calls home were limited, the cost was surprising. I tried hard to respect her privacy, but this time I had to break that trust. The same number appeared several times a day, both incoming and outgoing. It was the same as on our previous trip to Europe. I wanted to confront Pantea, but my words would fall on deaf ears since her nature was to shout back and not listen nor discuss. So, I kept silent and let things be.

In years past, she was a party girl, but since we got together, she had limited her drug use, stopped drinking, and reduced her partying. Not to mention, she had left her so-called work. She had changed totally; she was completely attached to me. I didn't know whether this was as a permanent client or a lover. But, for me, it was pure love, nothing else.

I understood she wanted her freedom and I never expected her to be a shut-in. My intentions were to have Pantea by my side completely.

Chapter Twenty-Four:

Pantea was Delighted

On December 14, 2015, a wedding for my third daughter was arranged. I, of course, wanted Pantea to join us, although I was hesitant to ask. Thankfully, she had met my other two daughters and agreed to come along. I was excited, but she was bringing Anahita. She would not come alone. I reluctantly agreed, knowing it was the only way to have her attend. Then, a few days before the wedding, Anahita injured her foot and canceled. I figured Pantea would decline when she'd have to come alone. However, to my surprise, she still came.

Pantea wanted to buy some Indian sarees before the wedding, so we made a shopping date. We went to some designers and she bought two of her choice, but Anahita persuaded her to buy another saree from Mumbai for the wedding day. I took Pantea to a jewelry shop owned by a school friend in Santushi. She selected one piece, and later one particular pair of earrings caught her attention. She was hesitant and worried I would be upset about her shopping spree, so she set it aside. In the background, I saw her attraction, so I picked up the earrings and put them her hand and closed her hand, saying, "This too, please. I like this one."

The next day we agreed to meet around twelve o'clock since later that afternoon was one of the functions. I arranged a hairstylist and manicurist to come at 2 pm. Pantea would meet her at the hotel.

Pantea was a VIP guest at my daughter's wedding, although she never liked anyone doting on her especially when it came to my children. Pantea was a very thoughtful person and did not want me to chase her in any way. Later that afternoon, I went to her room, and she offered me a quickie; I agreed. However, I never appreciated making love quickly. But Pantea always looked after me, even though it was never love on her part. I could not understand her reasoning in this respect.

Pantea arrived dressed in a saree, looking gorgeous. Rozhan met her at the entrance of our farmhouse. My wife welcomed her with open arms, but Pantea was very nervous. Then I introduced her to Shabhu, my third daughter, the one who was getting married.

I instructed my children to watch over Pantea during the ceremony since she told me not to come near her during the gathering. So, I watched from afar.

Pantea did some dances at the party, and Rozhan commented on how well she danced. It was difficult to keep my distance, as she was so beautiful. Pantea stayed an appropriate amount of time and left for the hotel.

The ceremony continued the next evening, with about a thousand guests. The event was organized by my eldest daughter, Meenaa. I am proud of her organizational skills. I was busy most of the day, and then at about 4 pm, I went to Pantea's room for about an hour.

I met Pantea at the Boy's Barat. When she walked in, I watched her as she graciously moved down the long walkway like a princess. It took about two hours to complete all the rituals. Shortly after, I noticed Pantea standing with Dr. Anuja. He was my dermatologist, and she had also taken treatment with him on my suggestion. They knew each other from the times she visited his office for some Botox and filler appointments, which we went to together.

We had various Russian girls dancing, along with a DJ and a famous singer named Akhid with a band named Naha.

The party was a complete success. Pantea enjoyed herself immensely. Shortly after Akhid and Naha finished, my daughter Meena and some other guests wanted more songs. So, Meena made the request to me through Pantea for more songs and requested Akhid to sing longer. My quest for the band to perform an encore was a success. Pantea was delighted I was able to achieve my goal. The party went well into the early morning. I knew Pantea left at about 2 am. We met in Mumbai the next week; I was grateful she had a nice time. It made my heart gleam when she was happy. The time went well because Anahita could not come. Otherwise, she would have had some criticism of me to pass along.

Chapter Twenty-Five:

I Was Facing the Music

Before our next visit, Pantea was having trouble finding the mascara she liked, so I made a trip to Vasant Kunj Emporia. But, during my visit, I called to ask which one she wanted. After she confirmed I bought three. It was January 26th, 2016, at 3:15 pm. At that time, she told me she was at the gym, after which she was going grocery shopping. At 3:30 pm I called again, but there was no answer. Finally, I asked if she was still at Nature's Basket. She did not reply until 9:40 pm, which was unusual.

She finally responded, "I don't have to be in touch with you every minute of the day, nor am I required to tell you my whereabouts at all times." I knew something was fishy.

It was later revealed that she was having an affair with doctor Shesha from 3:30 until 9:30 pm at her home, a place

I was not allowed to enter. This came to my attention at a later date.

During our conversation, I asked if we could meet on Sunday, the next day.

Pantea agreed, and I booked the next flight at twelve o'clock. "I will see you at 4 pm."

I struggled to understand why she would want someone else. We never had any commitments and she could see anyone she chose, however, with me her needs were always met. I had gotten to know Pantea and her character; she hated the call girl work and as long as she remained with me it was a life she could leave behind. As the man in her world, she could always rely on me to assist her with anything. As she stated many times, I was her hero.

We met on Sunday, but something was wrong. It was obvious her mind was in another place. I knew she was not my normal girl. Pantea had her own thoughts, along with a certain way of doing things.   She told me many times she cheated on her boyfriends all the time.

Pantea always said she could not commit to one person: "If I wanted to pledge myself and get married, I would have all the comforts of life."

She told me clearly that she would never be bound to anyone in life, a statement she made from the very beginning. She was never bothered by money or the future. Pantea lived on the edge. But I was in love and did everything to make her happy. Many times, she told me, "If we are together, it's only because of you."

Pantea did not forget about anything I'd done on her behalf, but she had a difficult time showing any appreciation. In my thoughts, she was number one. Unfortunately, she never realized the extent of my love. I believe in her heart of hearts, Pantea was attached to me and loved me more than she realized.

The following week again, Saturday afternoon, she went missing from 3:45 pm till 9:40 pm. It turns out she was with Dr. Shesha in her home again. They were making love for that time. The whole incident was confusing; Pantea was not that girl any longer, nor the one who didn't call or respond.

My only reasoning was love; she must have been infatuated with Dr. Shesha. But then what was my role? I was broken-hearted. However, I could see the guilt written all over her face. I knew Anahita would give her a boost; she made her feel at ease. Since there was no answer on Saturday, I left

Sunday morning, around 10:00 am, for Mumbai and called her from the airport.

She was very upset, "Why did you come? I did not reply with a confirmation."

Pantea had forgotten about my last message explaining my arrival on Sunday.

She finally said, "Okay, I will see you at 5:00 pm."

At the end of January 2016, her mother was coming to visit. But, during that time, I received a strange call from someone in Mumbai.

The caller stated, "I know Dr. Shesha's wife and she asked me to contact you. Pantea is meeting with Dr. Shesha Jay regularly."

I abruptly replied, "Thank you for contacting me, but I am not sure how to handle the situation. It's her life and I have no control over what she does. She is a director of my company, and it's personal life."

"As a director of your company, it's not good business practices. She is going to give you a bad name. Besides, Dr. Shesha is married with two daughters and their family will be ruined. She sees him every Saturday at the apartment. Plus, his wife knows of the affair."

I was confused and found it hard to believe. But I did not know how to handle the situation. The circumstances left me altered. One day, I saw my daughter Praful using some homeopathic liquid sleep drops and came up with a solution. I went to the market, and the next time I met with Pantea I would put it in her food. While she was sleeping, I could scroll through her phone and find out the truth. In the event I had to confront her over the situation, I had to have proof. Otherwise, she would completely deny everything. The last thing I wanted to do was lose Pantea, and living with the doubt was unbearable.

My plan was not without risk, and I knew it was a bad idea, but desperation causes people to do crazy things. Pantea wanted to visit Delhi the day before her mother arrived, but she had to leave on the last flight as her mother was coming the following afternoon. We ordered some lunch, paneer Penini, around 5 pm in the hotel suite. While she was in the restroom, I grabbed the drops and tried to put some in her food, but she came back sooner than expected, and caught me putting the drops in her meal.

In the heat of the moment, I panicked. "What are you doing?" she shouted.

"I was putting soy sauce on your meal."

She went to the food trolley. "Show me what you used. I don't know what you have been putting on my food all this time." She threw the bottle.

Pantea was very upset over what I did. She kept shouting; it made me feel very ashamed. The situation left me at a loss for words. I listened quietly while she yelled.

After she calmed somewhat, she grabbed the bottle and dumped the entire contents on my lunch and demanded I eat it. There was no other choice but to eat, which I did. But the drops had no effect; maybe my anxiety reversed the effects - or maybe it was useless being homeopathic medicine, as they are very light medications. She shouted at me again, wondering why I did it.

I told her, "You wanted to take a late flight today, and I wanted you to sleep so that you can go on a morning flight."

My explanation was not accepted, she did not believe a word I said. I did not realize how well Pantea knew me, better than I thought. She could see right through me, but I had to keep my reason secret. I was so upset that she was seeing someone at her home every week, making love to him, and I was never allowed to come over. The circumstances looked bleak; I had lost her for good.

Pantea left immediately after the incident and called Anahita on the way to the airport. Then she called Millin, all the while thinking I was poisoning her or something. It was impossible to convince her otherwise at this point. I had to accept the punishment for my actions. I knew deep down I'd lost her for good this time. The only option was to figure out the truth: Was she having an affair with Dr. Shesha? I kept apologizing, but she wouldn't respond.

After a few weeks, I requested that she meet on February 14, 2016, for a few hours. Somehow, she agreed to meet with me for two hours, since her mother was visiting until the end of the month.

I went to Mumbai and stayed at the JW Juhu. We agreed to meet around 1 pm. She brought some gifts and a card that said, "The little joys that become beautiful memories. The many treasures that my heart can hold, you are the most precious gift of them all. Every little thing you do makes me fall in love with you … Even little things you say swiftly take my breath away… Wishing you health and wealth in your life. You are my rose valentine."

 I wanted her to punish me, but on the other hand, I was upset about the situation with Dr. Shesha. Pantea stayed for three hours, and we made love but as usual to her, it was just sex. We did not make amends; the incident left a black mark on our relationship. My actions were a way of protecting the woman I loved, but it meant taking the blame. I asked her how much money she needed to be comfortable.

I had 200,000 dollars in my mind, but she said, "100,000 dollars are sufficient. I am alone, what will I do with the extra money?"

I am sure Pantea did not discuss the money with Anahita, otherwise, she would have advised her to ask for 200,000 dollars. Wherever there was tingling mingling of Anahita, the drama was being stirred behind the scenes. I was facing the music because of Anahita's effects on Pantea, but she didn't believe me, so I had to stay quiet. Anahita was very dear to her heart.

Chapter Twenty-Six:

I Wanted to Protect Her Always

The situation continued to escalate. On the third week of February, a girl called me stating she was Dr. Shesha's girlfriend and had many things to discuss with me. According to the girl on the phone, Dr. Shesha was neglecting her and his wife.

I was getting irritated and told her firmly, "If you are Shesha's girlfriend, then control him. Besides, who am I to stop her actions? She is the director of my company and the flat is a business rental. I will not interfere with her personal life. Nonetheless, she would never entertain a man in her home. "

"Well, Dr. Shesha wants to get rid of her but she is blackmailing him."

I could not resist, "You have no reason to keep calling me with this stuff. Besides, Pantea would never do any such thing. She is a good person. Nor would she have an affair with a married man." I blocked her phone number from thereafter.

Under no circumstances was I going to lose my cool and make another mistake. However, I was upset Pantea refused to let me come to her home as I might invade her privacy. The one time I did come over she yelled at me. According to her, she did not want people seeing any man coming and going from her flat. But now, she had a man coming over once a week to have sex.

Pantea's mother left on March 1st, but Pantea requested two days to rest. We agreed to meet at the Taj Land Send Hotel after two days. My officer friend Mohamed was also visiting Mumbai, so she arranged to have someone meet with him and I booked a separate room for them. It was about 1 pm when Pantea showed up, but the tension remained strong. She appeared confused at various times. On multiple occasions, she went into the bedroom to talk on the phone, and the calls continued about every half hour. Some were from Anahita as well as others. It was apparent something was seriously wrong.

My friend arrived around 8 pm and his girl showed up at about 9 pm. We had drinks and he left shortly afterward for his room with his girl. Once he was gone, it was the first time Pantea and I had talked for several hours on such a different topic. I was surprised by the questions she asked.

After trying to make sense of her issue I told her, "Whatever is going on you can talk to me. I will help you with anything."

She calmly said, "No, there is nothing going on." Pantea just had some questions about a friend who was having an affair with a married man and his wife was informed of the situation. A reporter called her, saying that he was doing a story on them. He had asked several questions about her friend.

"I am confused about whether the media can write something like that."

In fact, I knew as the reporter had called me too and had asked me several questions, and I had decided to control it on my own through my known sources. Now I was sure I must do something about it.

"Yes," I told her. "The media can do anything they want." I reminded her of my story: "I was falsely accused and ruined by the media." Her questions made me wonder.

She still looked confused. "If your friend has a problem, let me know if I can help. I know a lot of people in the media and can get it controlled."

Anyway, my consoling was useless, as Pantea was very worried. Something was on her mind. She expressed concerns about the self-respect of her friend (although in fact, it was all about her) and that she had no one in this country to protect her except her few friends. My internal thought was I am here for you always, and will do anything to help. She was not opening up with me about the issue. Anahita was leading her with stupid, illogical information and Pantea followed blindly.

We stayed together that night and parted ways the next morning. The situation seemed fishy. It was my sworn duty to protect her in any way possible. I knew deep down the story was bullshit and concocted by a jealous person or someone related to the doctor, most likely his own wife.

The next day she left but I stayed behind without informing her to control the situation. I met the concerned reporter and explained the situation but he was adamant to do the story. He had a questionnaire prepared for all concerned with the story. I invited him for evening drinks and dinner which he agreed to.

After a few drinks, I offered him 1,000 USD. He gave me copies of the questions he had prepared to ask Dr. Shesha which read as follows: "Doctor is it correct you are married to Dr. Rupani? How many children do you have? You are having an affair with a girl named Lana. You make phone calls every day, sometimes from 6:30 am till midnight every day, at least six to eight times. Lana has given us her phone bills.

"Is it correct that you go to the 5Y gym every day at 5:30 pm and leave at 7:30 pm? You meet her there; the gym staff has confirmed you being there at those times.

"Is it correct that you go and meet at her apartment every Saturday between 3:45 pm and 9:30 pm? Lana has also confirmed this, and the security staff of the apartment building has also confirmed.

"Is it correct that she is having an affair with another man named Alborz who is also meeting her at her apartment every week? Lana has confirmed that you are aware of it.

"Is it correct that Lana also has videos of you recorded in her bedroom? She has confirmed you had promised to pay her a large amount of money for the last year and you have now declined to do so. She has agreed to expose you completely."

Lana had already been questioned when he confronted her the night before. So, I believed she was very nervous as he revealed the incident that took place with her, not with her friend.

The paper he handed overstated as follows, "Miss Lana, is it correct that doctor Shesha Jay is having an extramarital affair with you?

"Is it correct he calls you six to eight times every day, and you also call six to eight times every day? Dr. Shesha Jay has confirmed this and we have your phone bills.

"Is it correct that he meets you at the 5Y gym every day for two hours? This has been confirmed by Dr. Shesha and gym management also.

"Is it correct that you are also having an affair with a person called Alborz? This has also been confirmed by Dr. Shesha Jay.

"Is it correct that the doctor comes to meet you at 3:30 pm every Saturday at your apartment and leaves at

9:30 pm? We have entry registers and photos of him entering your apartment.

"What do you do with him in these six hours at your apartment? Dr. Shesha Jay has confirmed that he meets you for many hours each Saturday and sometimes on some other days as well.

"What does Dr. Shesha Jay pay you every visit?"

Incidentally, I realized he did not give any questionnaire for Dr. Rupani. However, I settled the matter and convinced him to not do the story for 2,000 dollars and never told Pantea (until now).

The only explanation that came to mind was Dr. Shesha wanted to break off the relationship and was using his girlfriend to cause a problem. But, in the four years of our relationship, I'd never seen her this nervous. Someone was causing turmoil, and it could be a number of individuals. Maybe one of her friends was jealous, Millin, Leela or Anahita. Nonetheless, for better or worse, for me Pantea was important and I had to deal with their friendship.

A few days later a large parcel was delivered to my office addressed to my wife, and the return address was Pantea's apartment. It was a parcel like a doctor's bag. I sent her a message and informed her of the package delivery.

She burst out, "Oh… so, you received one as well? But I did not send any courier. See what's in it."

I said, "It was delivered to my office as no one has my home address. Just wait, I'll call you later when I have it in hand."

I sent someone to get the parcel from my office, which I received a few hours later.

Then, I messaged her again, stating, "I have your package and will open it in about half an hour when I am done with my work."

Chapter Twenty-Seven:

Only Time Will Tell

Needless to say, the stress over the package's contents
was nothing in comparison to the reality of what I saw
when I opened the box. The phone calls I'd been receiving
were valid: phone records, photos, etc., filled the box. A
year of call records with Dr. Shesha Jay, pictures of him
entering Pantea's apartment. The whole incident was laid in
front of my face. Plus, the information about our
relationship had been addressed to my wife. I stared at the
contents in horror, my worst fears had come true. The calls
to Dr. Shesha were highlighted, occurring several times a
day from both sides. Then, there were pictures of him
entering the gym to see Pantea, and images of him parking
the car. I never imagined anything like this
happening. Each photo was described differently, as
follows:

Dr. heading to Berprings

Dr. entering Berprings and giving his name to security guards

Dr. parking the car at Berprings

Dr. parking the car at Berprings

Lana's car parked in the gymnasium basement

Dr. parking his car in the gymnasium basement where Lana is already sitting and waiting; Lana giving him a blow job in the car.

The letter that was addressed to Rozhan was as follows:

"Mrs. Azar,

"Your husband Alborz is having an extramarital affair with a girl called Lana in Mumbai. She is a foreign national. Your husband is meeting her every week in Mumbai.

"Lana's phone number is 9999999001. Your husband and Lana are in touch on her phone. Her total phone bill for a year is provided here, you can check. She is having an extramarital affair with Dr. Shesha Jay who works at a famous hospital.

"I have sent a letter to the doctor's wife too. Here are photos of the doctor going to Lana's apartment. I have not been able to capture your husband's photos since I do not know where they meet, but this information is correct. Your husband gives her USD 2000 per visit. Lana's address is F wing Apartment 602 BERPRINGS APARTMENT. She has five cell phone numbers.

"If you tell your husband or ask him then she will start using another cell number because he is fully trapped by her and he is desperate for sex with Lana. How do you propose to stop this?

"It is your choice if you want to report her to the police, if you want to meet her at her apartment without your husband and confront her, or if you want to catch them together red-handed, just go where your husband is staying in Mumbai."

"It's your call now. I can help you however possible. Call me at 7507625600. The newspapers have been informed too; they are going to do a story and I will send it to you."

The news story will publish as stated below:

"Doctor Shesha Jay, an orthopedic doctor at a famous hospital, is having an extramarital affair with Lana. Dr. Shesha Jay, a famous orthopedic consultant cum surgeon at a well-known hospital, is married to Doctor Rupani, head of the pathology department in a large hospital.

"It is reported that he is having an extramarital affair with a girl named Lana staying at Lokhand. It is reported that she went for treatment for her knee pain and then they started meeting every day, first from 7 am to 9 am and later from 5:30 pm to 7:30 pm at the 5Y gym near Berprings and the hospital where the doctor works.

"It didn't end here there: He promised her a big lump sum of money and wanted the bedroom to satisfy his sexual hunger by going to her apartment for sex every week as reported by sources. The documents prove him being seen at her apartment and phone bills of Lana provided by her itself.

"As per the phone bill, he calls her five to twelve times every day. It is also reported by sources that he is paying Lana every visit.

"But when he did not pay the promised lump sum, Lana recorded him on video at her apartment and she provided her phone bills and entry registers to this bureau.

"Upon contacting the doctor, he stated she is also having an affair with someone named Alborz who also comes to her home. Lana refuses to comment on this. Upon contacting the 5Y gym, they confirmed that both Doctor Shesha Jay and Lana come at 5:30 pm and leave together at 7:30 pm.

"The point is these are our professional doctors and detract from patient confidentiality. Shame on such doctors. And shame on such gyms like the 5Y that allow extramarital affairs to go on in the gym."

I loved Pantea more than me myself. She was my life, my power, my inspiration. The only other person who ranked higher was Rozhan. I would have died for her provided there was a good reason. My love was unconditional, she is a lovely girl in all respects. It was a passion beyond words.

As I went through all the bills, images, and statements, attached to each photo were notes; it seems the doctor's wife was spying and took the pictures. Pantea was very upset, and I think she was embarrassed over the situation, especially since they sent the package to me exposing their relationship. I kept quiet while she shouted about the incident, but later when she called back in tears, I accepted her apology.

Then Anahita took the phone, "She is young, Alborz. It's easy to fall into such a situation. Pantea is crying and telling me she can't face you anymore. She's wondering how you can forgive her when you have done everything for her," Anahita said. "I have told her to go and meet with you."

"Tell her to come and we will talk and sort everything out," I replied.

"When should she come?" Anahita asked.

"I will get a flight for her tomorrow, and she can meet you in Delhi."

Pantea came to Delhi and I could see she was very guilty over the situation. She explained it was a random affair. It started when she went to see him for knee pain at the hospital, and then he kept sending messages to meet. She believed his wife was the culprit and caused the incident. Dr. Shesha thought there was a third person. Pantea told me they met four times. He was afraid to be seen outside with her, so they met at home. As she explained, their affair only lasted for four weeks, but he sent her several messages to meet and she fell into his trap. In fact, I thought Pantea did not owe me any explanation; she was an independent girl, which was why she never planned to marry. But she would never forget the good things I had done for her; she was not a harami girl.

As she explained, "His wife has a boyfriend who works at HDCD bank. Can you get his wife's cell details for one year?"

"Yes, I'll call a guy who I know, who can do it for 400 USD."

In my opinion, she was asking all these questions because of Anahita. Anyway, I promised her the required information would arrive next week when I came to Mumbai. What I did not know was our discussion were being passed along to Dr. Shesha.

We agreed afterward that the discussion was over and we would not speak of it again. But the doctor's wife would not let the incident end anytime soon. Rupani went with Dr. Shesha to all her sources to implicate Pantea in whatever way they could. Then she went to her husband and they went to the police and filed a complaint against Pantea.

Then they hired a lawyer, but Dr. Shesha never said anything against Pantea. He just said they had an affair.

The doctor's wife requested the police commissioner to file a complaint against Pantea for blackmail. Dr. Shesha confessed to the police he was with Pantea from 3:00 to 9:30 pm. But the commissioner refused since the doctor had already admitted to the affair as his photographs showed him entering the apartment building. Besides, she did not demand any money. A lawyer called Pantea, but she refused to speak with her on the phone. Pantea made me return the call to call the lawyer, who did not pick up. I left a message.

Apparently, several packages were couriered, and his two daughters were working with his wife against him. A very close friend of his wife working at HDCD bank had given her Pantea's account details and had hired the reporter. I expressed my distaste for the situation and asked if Pantea would give me the phone numbers and I would take care of the problem.

Rupani's lawyer called me the next day. We discussed Pantea's position in my company. She was innocent and couldn't be blamed for anything. I was told she mustn't contact Dr. Shesha any longer, because his wife said they were still in communication. The accusation was false and his wife was fabricating stories.

In March 2016, the doctor's wife made her husband resign from the hospital he was working at and he moved to another famous hospital. From there, he left the gym and stayed clear of Pantea. They stayed in touch but not as lovers. They had some feelings left for each other, which is obvious since it was not a short affair; it had lasted for about two years.

But, frankly, the incident left me crushed. My heart was broken. She allowed a stranger into her home, and I was not allowed near her home. They had been engaging in sexual encounters every Saturday while I was left in the dark. I had to keep silent or she would have left immediately. My worst fear was losing the love of my life. I had the option to find other girls, but I wanted to be with Pantea.

The stress left me restless; I could not sleep or concentrate. I felt alone but shared the problem with Rupali, who tried to console me. However, her advice did not help as it was in favor of Pantea which left me desperate. I refused to believe that Pantea went looking for someone else intentionally, however; she is young and the advances of a doctor were appealing. Maybe she fell in love. But the real question was, WHO DID IIT.

Who exposed the affair to all? It could have been a number of people, including one of her friends who was jealous of her comfort and good life. Leela who was no longer friends with Pantea? Milin who was jealous, although she was always willing to lend a hand? Anahita, a trusted friend, or is she? The doctor's girlfriend? Rupani, the doctor's wife who wanted to save her family? Rupani's boyfriend working at the bank, trying to win his girlfriend's favor? Maybe someone who did not want Pantea to be with the doctor or me? Or perhaps an unknown conspirator?

My resolution to figure this out will be exposed in the sequel to "WHO DID IIT."

All readers may try to answer this question and send their guess; the first 100 people with the right answer will be sent to the next book "I Did It" free of charge. One guess per person, please. The next book will be published soon. All responses are confidential.

Author Bio

Alborz Azar has been dubbed a hero by Pantea (Lana). The story is narrated by Alborz who was once called a great hero by the woman he loves. However, she declined to be titled as the author. In light of the situation, she chose to avoid involvement due to his family. Pantea would go on to call Alborz Azar Casanova, Marco Polo, her hero, etc.

Azar faced all the situations in his life with confidence and believed in the truth. The luxuries in life that he procured were due to his dedication to succeeding in business. They were not inherited from any family legacy.

The struggle to overcome all his difficulties with persistence started at the age of fourteen, but he found his passion for work and dedication drove him to succeed. However, he is still waiting for a successful conclusion in his long-drawn-out litigations for his legal rights. As time passed, his first love was his wife Rozhan continued to stay at his side. Thereafter, some lovely girls crossed his path; the most important was Pantea.

Azar's dream to become a successful entrepreneur started at a young age. His drive to achieve a name in the corporate world was achieved to an extent, but he was held down by some dirty business rivals in false acquisitions. In the foreseeable future, his complete life story will be written in hopes it will touch the hearts of his readers.

Epilogue

Eshgham helped Alborz understand that what he thought was love was not the same as I love you, but more like I love you in my manner.

Alborz learned how two people should treat each other, in the continuing saga of Alborz and Pantea. WHO DID IIT is a true love story of someone who still lives for his Eshgham, but she does not believe in love? Nonetheless, in the second book, the tides change, as she starts saying I love you to Alborz.

However, just when he thinks all is well with Pantea, Alborz makes a horrible mistake, and she completely stops saying I love you. In the third book, Pantea finds a way to forgive Alborz and says I love you once again, only the message is masked by Pantea's unique personality.

CPSIA information can be obtained
at www.ICGtesting.com
Printed in the USA
LVHW022225081221
705652LV00012B/191